# SOULS IN EXILE

# SOULS IN EXILE

A collection of short fiction
by

## NICK PADRON

Adelaide Books
New York / Lisbon
2020

SOULS IN EXILE
A collection of short fiction
By Nick Padron

Published by Adelaide Books, New York / Lisbon
adelaidebooks.org

Editor-in-Chief
Stevan V. Nikolic

For any information, please address Adelaide Books
at info@adelaidebooks.org
or write to:
Adelaide Books
244 Fifth Ave. Suite D27
New York, NY, 10001

ISBN: 978-1-953510-71-6

Printed in the United States of America

*For Lourdes, as always*

# Contents

# Sylvia's Island

*a novelette*

Sylvia sat gazing at the muscular specimens swaggering past the Le Belvedere beachfront. They came marching ever closer to the fire bush hedges, high-stepping on the sand like prize horses, their black bodies glistening in the sun. I made my way through the lounge chairs under the tiki-hut, a sultry mix of sulfur and Chanel Number 5 wafting in the air.

A few of our fellow shade-worshipers had taken up positions alongside the bordering hedge to better appraise and be appraised by the sand-walkers. I climbed the wooden deck that doubled as a bandstand to Sylvia's reserved spot. We greeted each other, she with her languid, "How are you, darling."

With the towel neatly spread over the chair, I reclined beside her, our figures in full tropical regalia — flowing semi-transparent, peek-a-boo red and green materials revealing, obscuring what was there of us.

Sylvia extended her short vein-free legs, whiter than the sand on the beach, and slipped her skirt up to her thighs for effect. She knew how her white skin attracted their eyes.

"They're coming closer," I said.

"It's almost noon, my dear." Sylvia picked up her Bloody Mary, gold bracelets jingling.

"Ah," I said. "Lunchtime — right."

"You're learning." She winked at me from behind her wide-lens sunglasses.

Although I couldn't imagine Sylvia having any idea as to what it would be like to be food hungry, I had to agree, feeling rather pleasantly corrupt myself, I was learning. One by one, every lounger in the hotel's garden became the staging platform to a different Blue Ribbon lady, posed to magnetize. Lady Bismarck came working her way toward the garden, beating the floor with a walking cane. She waved our way and sank herself onto the cushions of the nearest chair. She uttered something I didn't understand until Sylvia answered loudly, "Yes. Lovely weather," then under her breath, "At least she notices it."

"A day for the races," Lady Bismarck screeched from her chair.

Sylvia sighed. "Some boy out there is going to earn his tip today."

On the beach, it was hot and bright, full of physical activity.

A couple of early birds had already gotten up and disappeared with their catch. The procedure was pretty straightforward. A smile or a wink would alert the sand-walker that he'd been picked and to proceed to the hotel's side door, where a uniformed staffer would give him a final inspection and escort him to the guest's room. Everyone observed the rules. We were also free to arrange our own trysts, the same as any guest outside the plan. But none of the Blue Ribbon ladies ever chose this option, too much of a waste of time. Besides, few dared to set foot outside the hotel's boundaries on their own.

I thought of giving it a try on my own, as a personal statement of independence. It seemed the least I could do was to take a closer look at the boy before moving on. But one time was all it took for me to yield to the norms. Any observance of convention, the same as any wish for self-reliance, seemed pointless in the extravaganza of carte blanche privileges afforded to us Blue Ribbon ladies.

I had found this beach town's little secret through research I'd been doing for a new client last year, an international consortium interested in building a luxury resort on the Hispaniola Island. During the study, I came across a New York Times report on rich American women who flocked to the Caribbean to get their 'groove back,' which mentioned Le Belvedere's Blue Ribbon plan. At a department meeting, I proposed Le Karakol area as a possible location for the resort. Building in Haiti presented some unique opportunities I believed to be most favorable to the developers. To my secret surprise, my suggestion was approved and included in the list of possible sites — a win for me and my team. Later on, the notion of regaining one's groove hit me in full as too great a temptation. So the day after Christmas, I got on the phone and made a reservation. The hotel delivered the travel documents by courier to New York a week later. I told no one about it except my sister Deb, whose response was, "Are you crazy? You're looking to get rape — or worse?" In any case, on Epiphany Day, I took the three flights, the planes getting smaller at every connection until we landed at a nearby field outside the town.

Seen from the potholed road, Le Karakol could easily pass for an African village on the other side of the world. Multicolored taxi-pickup trucks zipped through unkempt alleys of zinc-roofed shacks; women with baskets on their heads and farm animals meandered in the equatorial heat haze. There were none of the usual attractions for the typical surf and turf vacationer. As far as I could see, the town had nothing to offer an outsider besides its tropical isolation and, of course, Le Belvedere's body trade singularity.

The hotel's unwritten policy, which allowed the guests on the Riban Ble plan to remain anonymous, was one of its magical attractions. The government-issued document with the blue ribbon gave the guest a kind of diplomatic immunity for the duration of the stay. We were not required to turn in our passports, not even at the two shacks they called the airport. It was like not being in Haiti at all, if ever the need for denial arose.

On arrival, the manager at the reception desk handed me a pink card with a number like a nameless Swiss bank account. He asked me for an alias of my choosing, the name the staff and others would use when addressing me — an additional level of confidentiality that the guests particularly delighted on, he said. I told him to pick one for me to avoid having to guess the possible pros and cons.

"How about Mademoiselle Delphine?"

"Miss Dolphin?"

"It also means delphinium, a bluebell flower. A very chic name in French. Balzac used it in two of his novels."

"Oh, well, in that case—"

It would have been easy to be cynical and hide what was so much in the open in Le Belvedere. But that was just how it was. Middle-age-plus, wealthy American women seeking 'holiday romances' in poverty-stricken lands. I could sense the weight of it passing by me in the carved-wood paneled lobby and in the private obsessions lazing under the palm trees in the garden. I knew what to call it, but I hated it, hated the sound the words made in my head. But I went with it. Wasn't that why I'd paid a bundle to be here? To go with it?

On the sand, it was rush hour for the hungry sand-walkers. They paraded past us in their raggedy shorts, red and yellow the predominant colors, awkward young boys, men with huge smiles like children. Some tried to give off a sense of formality, heads bowing as they pass, carrying themselves as if applying for a job. The show-offs, the cartwheel-performers, the tongue-lapping clowns, them, we blocked off. We looked for the confident ones, Sylvia and I. For the ones naturally overloaded with sexual cachet and a touch of mystery — the ones Sylvia commented on only if I brought it up first — even if as a whole, they looked almost identical.

"How about him?" I said of the one circling back, pretending to be looking at his wristwatch.

"If you go for the type," Sylvia replied with a ghost of a shrug. "Oh, will you look at him over there," she said, stifling a giggle with her jeweled fingers over her lips. A broad-shoul-dered sand-walker was standing by the surf stripping off his rags in full view of the guests. When he was down to something that looked like a loincloth, he ran splashing into the water.

"Is he allowed to swim here?"

"Why not? They do everything but breathe in that water."

"Not much of a striptease," I said.

Sylvia gave me an all-knowing grin. "Darling, it's all promotional. You'll see why when he comes out sopping wet in those undies."

We looked at each other and laughed.

Just then, a boy in spandex shorts that left nothing to the imagination halted by the hedges. He squinted in our direction. I glanced over at Sylvia. She was fondling the sweat off her Bloody Mary glass. We couldn't tell whose chair he was focusing on. It didn't matter. It wasn't his choice to make. He paced under a palm tree near Lady Bismarck's lawn chair. She switched her beach bag to the opposite side. Useless caution, Sylvia said. The hotel had an armed guard somewhere tasked with dealing with any violations, but his presence would've been symbolic. The borderline between the hotel and the sand was secured by a greater more fearsome force. That of President-for-life Duvalier and his too-real Tonton Macoute henchmen, the secret police, a thing of wide-eyed horror to non-guests.

Two boys in matching net shirts stood facing my way now. My heart began to pound. I hated the feeling and tried not to show it. "It's hard to tell who they're looking at with those cheap sunglasses," I said to make Sylvia feel there was no competition between us.

"Oh, my dear, they'll take anything they can get."

When the sunlit boy in the spandex shorts came by again he halted, turned his skin-tight body, and looked away at the ocean with an air of carnal defiance. A signal of some kind? I wondered.

Sylvia's slight grin set a process in motion. A black-vested waiter appeared as if she had snapped her fingers. She pulled a ballpoint pen and a notepad from his pocket, slowly wrote a few words on the page and gave everything back to him. The waiter approached the boy on the sand, gave him some verbal instructions, and the boy walked off in the direction the waiter pointed with his arm. He made sure to watch the boy for a moment, nodded, and came back to the table.

He spoke Creole to Sylvia, which I didn't understand. The whole transaction seemed to have an extrasensory quality. She paused, thinking. "Rele Daniel," she said with a single nod.

Daniel was the tuxedo-donning hotel man who accompanied her whenever she called, her personal valet, his full-time job. He helped her up and they walked away together, the somber skeletal Haitian in black holding her fleshy ivory arm across the small lobby and into the tiny elevator — the dumbwaiter, Sylvia's name for it.

After a late lunch, I took a recovery nap and later went out to the garden. A hot breath blew on my face the instant I stepped outside the door. On the beach, only the gulls and the most desperate sand-walkers were out now. Nora, the widow from West Palm Beach, and Gabriella, the former Mexican beauty queen — both part of Sylvia's clique — were sitting together with their backs to the beach. I took the table beside theirs.

Hi . . . hi . . . hello . . . For a few moments they remained silent, processing my presence. I asked about Sylvia. Nora, who at times acted like Sylvia's lieutenant, said she didn't expect her to come down. Sylvia had vanished to her siesta — as she called her midday rounds — and wouldn't be back until evening.

"How long have you known Sylvia?" I asked Nora.

"Oh, we met four years ago, when the plan started." She wiped her abundant blonde-streaked hair off her long face revealing diamond stud earrings of at least two carats each. "We keep in touch in the States, too."

"She's quite a character," I said of Sylvia. "An interesting lady, for sure."

I glanced at Gabriella in her floral off-shoulder sundress, her round face made up as if for a night at Studio 54. I posed the same question to her.

"We met last December," she said with her Mexican inflections. "Not here. In the airport in New York. Our flight was delayed because of a big snowfall. We hit it off — you know. We found we had a few things in common, yes." She grinned and gave a little shrug with her shapely tanned shoulders. "She was the one who told me about the plan. Now it's my second time here — I have a friend coming in, too. But yeah, she is one colorful person, that Sylvia. God bless her. Unique. Says the craziest things sometimes. And you'll never beat her on stamina, no, no. You must've noticed how the boys look at her. They're scared of her." She laughed. "But they won't dare skip on her, either. If they know what's good for them."

"Oh, Gabriella," said Nora. "Don't you think you're exaggerating a little?"

"Yeah, maybe. But only a little. You," she said to Nora. "You know that better than anybody."

"Yes, I know. She does confide in me about some things. But what Sylvia tells me in private" — Nora gestured as if zipping up her lips — "stays between us."

I looked away wondering why she'd bothered to bring it up at all. I supposed being in with Sylvia of Le Belvedere carried a measure of distinction worth flaunting.

"Put it this way," Nora resumed. "Thanks to Sylvia, what happens in Le Karakol never happened. That should tell you everything." She drank to it.

I did too. "I'm all for that."

"That's why they treat her like a queen," Gabriella went on. "One word from her and that person is out of here, guest or visitor. It's happened. And she's picky," she added, mockingly extending the last syllable.

"So she's careful of who stays here and who she falls asleep with," Nora said. "So what?"

"Who isn't?" I said.

"But you're not paying someone to keep an eye on you all the time," Gabriella said. "She's got that penguin of a man on duty all day, catering to her. It's creepy. It's too much. Don't you think? I mean, any of us could hire a bodyguard or whatever, too."

"Oh, not me," Nora said. "I wouldn't relax knowing somebody's behind me all the time. God! Could you?"

I couldn't work myself to judgment. Although Le Karakol did hold an element of menace when I thought about it, at no time had I felt my security threatened. The boys could be intimidating up close. Alone with them behind locked doors, it never failed to scare some part of me. But it wasn't dread. Eye to eye, it was hard to ignore who they were. Men, boys, whose hunger made them travel miles for a chance to give the white mammas what the white mammas came for and live for a few hours the lives they'd only seen from the distance or on a TV screen. Few earned more than a meal and a tip, a bonus depending on their performance, and the generosity of the white mamma that had picked him. Most were let go with the equivalent of a Haitian week's salary and a story to tell, or a secret to keep. Whatever it was the boys found in the soft white skin of women old enough to be their mothers, or their grannies, was a touchy subject among the guests at Le Belvedere — unless an unavoidable need to brag became too strong. I couldn't form an opinion of the locals as easy as the others could. From my perspective, we were the ones they had to fear.

That evening Sylvia, Nora, and I sat together in the hotel's restaurant. Thinking it an interesting topic over the dinner table, I brought up my company's plan to build an international resort in the area. I regretted it the moment I said it.

"A vacation resort?" Nora said, her bronzed mask furrowing to its foundation, horrified. "My God! Did you hear that, Sylvia?"

It threw Sylvia into a sinister silence.

"You must do something to stop it," Nora went on as if I had any influence over the matter. "You've got to try. I mean, it would ruin everything . . ."

I was well aware of the impact an international resort with all its trappings would have on Le Karakol and the hotel's shady services. I just hadn't expected their reaction. I wondered what I was missing. I had come here for the same reasons they had, there was no hiding that — when you're a high forty-something American pale-skinned woman with a budget and not much to look at, the only reason to come to Le Karakol was clear. I just couldn't imagine this piece of jungle by the sea being anything other than something to put behind you once you left it. There was so much wrong about it. But detesting, as I did, being cast as a messenger of doom, I tried to dampen the shock.

"Ah, come on, guys," I said as cheery as I could make myself sound. "No point in worrying about that. These projects can take years to complete, if they happen at all. And by then, there'll be greener beaches to go to. Wouldn't you agree, Sylvia?"

I went to bed hoping she did.

In the morning the sun came out, a fiery force slashing through the room's half-opened blinds, the night gone forever but for its leftovers. Letting the madness off the leash had its consequences, the hangover being only one. I took a long shower and went downstairs to another sun-drenched day in Le Karakol.

Sylvia hadn't yet come down. So I waited by the veranda, having a cup of ginger tea. The rasped murmurings of the previous night's affairs filtered through the dining room window. The recently arrived were louder and peppier. I caught the occasional oh-my-god and the usual giggling descriptions of the boys' vitality and dimensions — together with the reluctant undertones of disgust at the way some fantasies crash in the face of reality. The morning longing for the touch of someone of your own, not of a rental, also filtered out in the quieter voices.

"Good morning, you," I heard Sylvia calling, her valet escort by her side.

"Hi." She seemed pleased to see me. I was glad about that. We walked together to the long table in the wraparound veranda where her coterie had gathered for breakfast.

I asked for The Queen's Breakfast on the menu. Sylvia glanced in my direction. I felt a comment on my appetite coming on.

"My, are we famished this morning."

"Missed dinner last night," I lied.

She assented with a silent vow of her head.

Afterward, the drinks came and the wait staff left us alone in the garden. Being Sunday, the sand-walkers were few and only the newcomers were by the fire bush shrubs watching them. It was hot, and I drained my rum special inside a fresh pineapple drink too fast, so I went to the bar for another. When I came back, Sylvia was holding court from her fan-backed wicker chair.

"Theoretically," she was saying, "the total of one hundred thousand men on each coast is all our country needs to serve the American woman. It's been studied and analyzed. One, two hundred thousand —"

"That can't be any good," Gabriella said. "We're millions of women. That would be horrible."

"Not to mention how bushed those poor men would be all the time," said Capri — short for Capricorn. "Sylvia, tell me you're not serious."

"I've read about it, too," Nora said. "It's a scientific theory. There's more to it than you think, I promise you."

"Please," Capri hissed. "There aren't enough men as it is."

"One hundred thousand men on each coast, distributed through every county or whatever," Sylvia went on. "The number of partners — we'll call them partners — will depend on the number of the specific female population in each area.

It's just an estimate, really, to illustrate how few are needed. Don't worry; there'd be as many men as necessary to take care of every woman's natural needs."

"Sounds like science fiction to me," I said.

"It's not fiction. If women were to own up to their place in the world, it could be done. It's a question of numbers. The calculations exist."

"Keep them like studs in stables nationwide? Hmmm," Capri hummed.

"Sounds like whorehouses to me," Gabriella said.

"Certainly not," Sylvia said. "We want the men to be useful, too. To have full lives while they're in the service. Eventually, they will retire the same as anybody."

"Oh, Sylvia." Gabriella laughed. "You have one fertile imagination, my friend. A little twisted — I mean that in a good way, of course."

"I do have an imagination, don't I?"

"And there'll be no other men? Only those?" I said to keep it rolling.

"Oh, we don't want all of them," Sylvia said, laughing. "Whatever for? The others can go about their business. This would be a service, an institution as any of old, for men of the right age and specifications to serve on active duty for their country. Are we not part of our country?"

"And how much will it cost?" Gabriella asked.

"Oh, I guess an administration fee would be in order — unless in dire situations. We don't want to seem un-inclusive."

"We wouldn't want that," Nora said, laughing.

None of the girls seemed inclined to call Sylvia's loveless fantasy what it was, insane, but I wasn't going to be the one to break the spell. I sort of let it drop, though, softly.

"That's one crazy idea, Sylvia," I said. "But hey, who's to say? It might work. When women rule the world."

Nora's eyes opened wide when she saw Sylvia's pallor harden.

"Oh darling, you just don't get it," Sylvia said, turning to me. "It's not about ruling the world — not right away, anyway. The problem is the number of men in our species. It's out of proportion with womankind. Unbalanced with nature. There are too many of them. And it's not going to get any better."

Capri cut in, "Unless it's changed, and I didn't hear about it, it's a well-known fact the female population is higher than men's everywhere."

"That's precisely the problem," Sylvia said, her collection of gold bracelets chiming. "Use your imagination. Think of studs on a farm." Sylvia smiled, but it wasn't a hypothetical question. "How many do you need? What would happen if you had more cocks than hens on a farm? What would a farmer with eight bulls for every cow get out of that arrangement?"

"Doesn't sound like a problem to me," said Gabriella in an attempt at humor.

"Busy livestock?" I said, joining in.

Sylvia let out a humorless laugh. "What you get is the world of man, ladies. Which is, by the way, where we all reside."

"So what are you saying?" I said. "Make an army of studs? Institutionalize male prostitution? Reduce the male population?"

Nora said, "I think she just means that men could be trained to serve women. Make it a trade like firemen or policemen. Right?"

"A career, why not?" Sylvia said delighted with the new spin on her idea. "I wasn't thinking of that. But who's to say? Something for boys to hope for. They'll love it. Trust me."

I looked at Sylvia's made-up face in the shade of the thatched-roof tiki, a perfect mask of Mary Kay, L'Oréal, Chanel products. It was hard to read her expressions behind her sunglasses. I wasn't sure if she truly meant what she was saying or it was her Bloody Marys or some other spirit talking. Every one of us Blue Ribbon ladies may have had our own dark little secret story, but the parts that showed all seemed to have something in common, an unburied madness, a hidden self-reproach, something denied for far too long. And Sylvia was no exception.

"Well," I said. "If anybody can do it, it's you, Sylvia." And she loved it, gave me a tap in the arm and a smile as a reward.

A sudden tropical shower erupted on the beach. I gathered my things quickly to get back indoors. Sylvia didn't stir, her cat-eyed gaze fixed on a speckle of islands out on the ocean, until Daniel came rushing with an open umbrella. She invited me to get under it with her and murmured in my ear. "You had two last night."

I felt the heat rising in my face. "What?"

"Oh, for God's sake." Sylvia's brows arched up. "It's none of my business. But my girl, what's the use? You know," she said, huddling closer under the umbrella. "That's what I like about you. You know how to keep things to yourself. You remind me of me. A little. Not looks-wise. I never had legs like yours or hair like yours."

"Nonsense," I said, ready to change the subject. "You have gorgeous eyes. They remind me of Elizabeth Taylor's."

"Oh yes, my eyes. My lone attribute. Every guy's opener when hitting on me. Not that it happened often. My good years were few and they didn't belong to me. I could've been born in a place like this and been better off, really. A gilded cage is still a cage."

"Had you been born here, you would've been president of the republic."

"You flatter me, darling," she said. "Though I would have rather it be a monarchy."

"And you the queen."

"Of course."

Listening to the rainfall in my room, I kept thinking of the conspiratorial tone in which Sylvia had brought up the issue of my two visitors last night. As if she'd noticed something about me that I myself didn't know it showed.

That evening, a new flight brought four new Blue Ribbon guests, Gabriella's friend among them, and the lobby was busier than usual. After dinner, I went straight to my room. I felt limp, nauseated from the meal, as though my body couldn't take any more abuse. From the night chambermaid, I was able to buy a couple of marijuana cigarettes, hoping for the kind of sleep the smoke gave me. I wanted to crash and not wake up until I could stand myself again. I brushed my teeth and was about to get into bed when I heard a soft knock at the door.

I was handed a handwritten invitation to have a nightcap with Sylvia in her suite.

I knew hers was the only suite in the hotel, and upstairs at the end of the creaking mahogany hallway, I found the door ajar.

"Come in, my dear." I heard her voice coming from the couch. "So happy you came. Close the door and sit over here." She was wearing a black sleeping gown that covered her from shoulders to ankles. Her feet were like a doll's, white with shiny red nails.

I sat across her on a cushioned bamboo chair, still feeling the smoke's influence. The room was twice the size of mine. It was crammed with suitcases and packed, store-like hanging racks; the top of the dresser was completely covered with jars, atomizers, and rows of perfume bottles. It did look like she lived in the room as I'd heard in the garden gossip. Rumors about her abounded whenever Sylvia wasn't around. That she was part owner of the hotel; that she had the local government in her payroll; that the sand-walkers belonged to her, hired and bred at a private stable she owned. And my favorite: that she was part of the same voodoo sect the President-For-Life belonged to, thus her influence in town. Did I believe them? Yes and no.

"Chardonnay? It's nice and fresh," she said.

"Thanks." My mouth was so dry.

She settled back with a regal pose, her legs up on the couch pillows. I didn't wonder for long what she had in mind. Of all the things that had gone through my head so far, I would've thought my job to be the last one. But that was what our private tete-a-tete was about to be.

"So your firm is looking to purchase land to build a tourist resort around here?"

"Not my firm directly. But, yes—"

"I did hear something about it from a friend in Port-au-Prince," she said. "How close are you to securing a deal?"

"It's still up in the air. They're leaning toward the Dominican Republic next door, a place called Samaná. A beautiful beach."

"I see," Sylvia took a sip of cognac and paused in thought, gazing at the night outside the window. Sitting under the overhanging lamp, she seemed older without her heavy makeup, tired, a strange brand of sorceress in a black silky puddle.

"You can't see them now because it's dark," she suddenly said. "But there's a group of islands out there. Maybe you've seen them during the day."

"I have. A couple of them."

"There are four in all, about three miles away. Nobody lives on the islands. On the one closest to the mainland, there are a few structures, ruins from an abandoned naval station built to fight German submarines during the War. Some of the local fishermen use it for storage, but not a soul stays in it. The locals say it's possessed by some unhappy deity." She paused with a grin on her tiny mouth. "I'm thinking of buying that island."

She looked my way to see my reaction. I smiled. "The whole thing? How big is it?"

"Twenty-some acres or so of useful land. A swamp of mangroves covers part of it. The rest is okay to build on as is."

"What do you have in mind to do with it?"

"Ah, that's the best part of it, darling. I see it as the birthplace of a new order."

"Wow."

She grinned as if saying, yes, I know it sounds crazy. "Maybe I'm getting a bit ahead of myself. Of course, it will begin with a private club. An idea of mine based on what I've learned from the Blue Ribbon plan. But," she said with her stubby index finger up, "infinitely better. Just imagine an entire island designed by experts for our particular interests, with lavish grounds and luxurious accommodations. That's what I'm planning to do with it."

"Pretty ambitious. Not just from the financial standpoint of a project of that size, but the nightmare it could be dealing with the government here."

"Very good," she said with a tone of surprise. "But I'm happy to say that isn't a nightmare anymore. Everyone and everything that had to be taken care of for the Amazonia Manor to operate on the up and up has been taken care of. Yes," She smiled, "Amazonia Manor, do you like the name?"

"Very feminine, in a way," I said.

"And you can guess who its members would be, can't you?"

"I can?"

"Of course, you can. Us! Women like the ones here." She leaned forward, her aquamarine eyes glittering with excitement. "In the beginning, it'll be a club and resort with a membership by invitation only, ultra-exclusive. Something like — and I hate to put it this way — a counter-play to Club Med and the Playboy club — the image of it that Heffner has made acceptable, but without the magazine. Our privacy rules wouldn't allow for that. We'll be merely borrowing the concept, turning it on its head, if you will, to conform to our needs."

"Something like the Playboy mansion, but for us girls?"

"Except in Amazonia Manor confidentiality would be sacred. Not like they do it, publicly showing off their celebrities and their bunny business." She sipped her drink with a devilish smile.

"Very impressive. Definitely not an enterprise for the faint-hearted."

"It's doable, love. That's what's important."

"So the club will come first."

"Yes. And it won't just be a nicer place to pick up sand-walkers either. It'll be much more than that. We will forge a philosophy," she said. "Just like the boys did, but more beautiful, because it will be ours. There are plenty of us to make it work, believe me. And when I say us, I mean women as ourselves who, for different circumstances, are alone — relatively speaking," she threw in with a grin. "But in a financial situation as significant as any of those big-shot bankers and crooked executives who rule our lives." She leaned closer as if to reveal a secret. "If we, just the few of us here now, were to manage our assets together as a group, let me tell you," her grin made her eyes sparkle, "our potential would be unlimited, my dear. There'll be no end to what we can do. We may be few, but — do you know what Lady Bismarck is worth?"

I had no idea.

"Her real name is Margaret Kapmann. The widow of Samuel Alfred Kapmann. Does it ring a bell? No? Well, she's good for at least a billion dollars. A billionaire! And she's right here with us. Now Gabriella," she said, nodding. "Yes, her, the Mexican Chihuahua. She's the eighth richest woman in her country. Can you imagine what a sisterhood of the likes of us could do if we're to join our resources, invest, create our own agenda?"

"An investment club for women only?"

"Oh, you make it sound so dull. Think bigger." She nodded at the window. "Amazonia Manor won't be just a private resort to come and get your groove back. It'll be so much more than that. Something such as the world's never seen. Not just made up of widows either, but of any independent-minded woman on the same level of affluence as us, powerful women who own their own destiny..." She stopped in mid-sentence, shaking her head in wonder. "I tell you, my mouth just waters when I think about it. Our possibilities are infinite."

"All I can say is, wow, Sylvia. From a resort to an empire." I raised my glass to her.

She shot me a side-grin. "I know you don't fit the profile. I know you're a working girl, ten, fifteen years younger than the average. But you could be a founding member if you're interested. In time, that'll be an important position, I promise you."

"Oh, Sylvia. Are you offering me a job?"

"No, darling, no. I'm offering you the possibility to be a collaborator. In what capacity? We can talk about it down the road. That island," she said pointing at the night, "will belong to me in less than a year. And then my Amazonian plan will begin." She downed her cognac, holding me in her gaze.

"Next year, huh?"

"All permits, licenses, certificates, all the paperwork has been completed and paid for in full. It's a tradition here. The government gets paid first. From the local Trou-du-Nord Arrondisement to the governor of the Nord-Est Department, to the President-for-Life and his police chief, they're all onboard. Everyone is interested in the success of this project. It's taken two years — believe me, it will happen."

"How much does an island go for in Haiti?"

"Not as much as the construction of the facilities, the cabanas, the main house, our offices, the help's quarters. Plus all that would come after the docks are rebuilt to start receiving supplies. There's nothing there now of use, except for the wells and a small landing field. We'd be starting from scratch."

"Who's financing this project, if I may ask?"

"Well, darling, I am," she said, settling back on the couch. She scrutinized me for a spell. "You don't think this is too crazy of me?"

She paused to give me time to take in what she had asked.

"I have to admit your idea is in the realm of fantasy for me. But I like it. It sounds like you have a strong vision of what you want to accomplish. There must be fortunes in untapped wealth out there in the hands of widows, in women in general, who might be willing to invest in a project of this magnitude. As for me, I can't wait to see it, of course."

She stood up, and I watched her refill her glass — the first time I'd noticed no one being around to do it for her. How many millions was she worth?

"Together," she said as she stepped back to the couch, "we could bring Wall Street to its knees. Not that we would do a crazy thing like that." She laughed as she settled back down.

Her madness was having an effect on me. Megalomaniacal as her idea sounded, it did seem to possess a touch of genius.

"I'm delighted you see it that way," she said. "Very pleased. So let me ask you this. How worried should I be about your resort project?"

Her bluntness shouldn't have surprised me, but it did. I said the first thing that came out of my mouth. "Well, it's not my project —"

"I know that. But your input carries some weight, or do I have that wrong?"

"It does, except the final decision is made by the client in Paris."

"I know that too. But the client counts on your firm's assessment to make the final decision as to the location, right?"

"Yes, in part — it's what they pay us for."

"A question: What would happen if your office were to downplay the benefits of building here, instead of in the D.R.?"

"I wouldn't know, really."

She paused and looked deeply into my eyes. "What would I have to do to keep your French resort away from here for, say, ten months to a year?"

I knew what she was driving at. I suddenly felt like running out of the room. "If the kind of thing you're asking me has ever gone on in my firm, it would've been handled upstairs. Way above my head and pay grade," I said, softly.

"What I'm asking you is," she said just as softly. "Is there a way that you'd be able to delay the decision for one year?"

A knot in my throat suddenly cut my speech.

"A year, my dear," she whispered. "One silly little year." All she needed was to hiss like a snake.

I remembered something like that happening once at the firm, when a conflict of interest surged between clients and a delay-maneuver was put into effect to benefit the principal account. But that was handled upstairs in the CEO's office, just as I'd told her.

"I wish I knew what to tell you, Sylvia. It has never even occurred to me to do anything like that. But I am flattered that you think I could help." I tried to laugh it off, blaming it on the drinks. "Boy, oh, boy. I must say, I didn't expect this tonight — not at all."

"Let me try to help you a little." Sylvia sat up. "I already know a few things about you. Not much. I know your name is." She halted with a playful smile. "Nancy. Nancy Barkley. You reside on Park Avenue and 69th Street — in a classic eight. You have an income of $80,000.00 a year, as a researcher, thanks to Granddad. You're a City College graduate. Took some courses at NYU. You've never married. You're forty-eight. You have a DUI in your —"

"What?" I jumped to my feet, shocked. "What the fuck, Sylvia," I said both furious and scared. Was I about to be black-mailed? "What's this all about?"

"Aaah, my dear, don't get like that, please. There's nothing sinister about this, I assure you."

"You know," I started to say, but choked on it. I put the glass down and stepped toward the window. I needed some air; I was so mad.

"Come now, sit down," I heard her say, her bracelets jingling, coaxing me to sit. "Please..."

I took a deep breath and sat on the edge of the chair. Now I needed to know what was on her shifty mind, for sure.

"Darling, listen to me. Don't get so upset. All the information I have is in the application you filled out for the consulate in New York. They passed it over to me. How else do you think I know about the others? Please. Here, have some of my cognac. Try it, it's delicious. Napoleon."

I tried calming down, hated the cognac. "You know, Sylvia, this really sucks. I was guaranteed our identities would remain secret. This is just —"

"And they are, just not to me. But they're safe with me, I assure you. Listen," she said, pausing to find the words. "There's so much we can do here for Le Karakol."

"Right now I couldn't care less about that."

"I know, I know." She brought me a glass of water and apologized in her sweetest voice while I sipped it. She continued talking, but I wasn't listening anymore. I was too upset and too much under the influence of the smoke and the alcohol to care about any of it.

" . . . Amazonia Manor will be so much more beautiful than anything we could ever dream of," her voice sounded as from a distance. "That island will be the one place in the world where women will truly rule, away from the influence of men . . . We're going to change things for all women. Trust me, we will . . . And I'd like you onboard with me, Nancy."

All I wanted to do was get out of there, so I just kept yessing her again and again as I moved closer to the door. "Sure. Yes, yes, I'll think about it . . ."

"Of course, darling. Of course," she kept repeating.

The only souvenir I brought back from Le Karakol was a blue orchid in a hand-painted little pot, a parting gift from the hotel. On my first day back at the office, I placed it on the windowsill next to the cactus. I had no hopes for a flower sitting on the twelfth-floor window over Madison Avenue in the dead of a Manhattan winter. But I'd been told this type of tropical plant grew in the air rather than in soil, something like Haiti itself.

A week later, I received a large envelope mailed from an address I didn't recognize in Port-au-Prince. It contained a series of Haitian official documents in Creole: a government gazette with a list of new zoning restrictions by Le Karakol's local government, a UNESCO study on the town's broken infrastructures describing the disastrous state of the roads and water supply system in the area. Along with a Parliament report on a proposed law raising taxes on foreign investments. It came without a personal note or instructions, but neither was needed. This was 'the material' Sylvia wanted me to include in my department's final report to discourage investment in Le Karakol.

The meeting of the department heads had taken place that afternoon. So I knew Sylvia would be calling this evening to find out how her little scheme had played out. It was almost midnight when my phone rang. I knew it had to be her. After a flash struggle whether to answer or not, I picked up the phone. I leaned on the window. Seven floors below, Park Avenue was bright with headlights in the wet night traffic.

"Sylvia, so nice of you to call."

"It's just wonderful to hear your voice, my dear. Have I called at a bad time?"

"No. It's okay."

"I've been in town for a few days. Are you surprised?"

"Oh yeah? That's wonderful, Sylvia."

"Yes. I came to do a little shopping and a little business. I'm looking forward to seeing you, darling. You will make some time for me, won't you? Perhaps on Sunday?"

"Absolutely."

"Oh, you're precious." She skirted the purpose of her call until we ran out of small talk. "So, tell me darling, how did it go in the meeting with the big boys?"

My spine froze when she finally uttered the words. I hadn't taken the Haitian reports to the meeting. I'd thrown the envelope in my desk drawer and left it there. I couldn't find the courage or see the sense in doing anything with it. Risk my professional life or worse, for Sylvia? No way. So I lied. I told her I'd done it. "It went well," I said. "The director agreed to pass it on to the investors."

"Uff." Sylvia let out a sigh of relief. "You have no idea the weight you've taken off my back, my dear. I shall never forget what you're doing for me — and our cause." She laughed her choppy laugh. "Oh Nancy, darling, your name will be on the plaque of the founding members of Amazonia Manor, no matter what happens from here on. So tell me, I heard the real big boys from Paris are scheduled to fly in this week. Is that right?"

How did she know that? "Yes," I said. "They're getting in on Thursday for the finals."

"Are you aware the three heads will be present? It'll be an all or nothing day for us."

I hadn't known myself all three of them would be coming until that morning; the fact that she knew, probably before I did, made the palms of my hands wet. "How did you get this information? If I may ask."

"Oh, my girl. It's our business to know. Isn't it?"

I didn't know what to say to that.

When Thursday dawned, I'd been up for hours. At eight, the taxi called from downstairs. By nine, I was in my office, a nervous wreck. The meeting was set for eleven. Mr. Campeu of Toronto was the first to arrive. I saw him from down the hall, being escorted to the drawing-room. My department chief called us in for a final run-through of our presentation. I had left the envelope with the Haitian material inside another envelope in my desk drawer. I just couldn't work myself up to touch it. I wasn't even sure of why I had lied about it to Sylvia. But I felt under no obligation to do anything for her. Her reaction on the phone, though, the way she'd shown her gratitude was now making me sick with guilt.

When they buzzed from the conference room, my associates put on their suit jackets. I stepped into my office for mine. I glanced at the Haitian orchid on the windowsill, its bluish, scarlet petals the colors of Sylvia's eyes. I opened the desk drawer and picked up the oversized envelope with the Haitian documents inside. I slipped it in between the files I was taking to the meeting.

In the hallway, Jonathan, my department manager, noticed my agitation. I told him I was worried about the clients signing the deal. "I really have my heart set on this one," I said in my most professional voice.

With the files against my chest, I walked by the long oval table in the center of the Conference Room. I glanced at the place cards on the polished tabletop. All the names Sylvia had mentioned on the phone were there. I took my seat next to Jonathan, behind our director's empty chair.

Waiting for the clients to come in, I kept feeling more and more layered away from the reality around me. I couldn't stop thinking about what The Belvedere had done to me. If Sylvia and the whole mad Le Karakol fantasy had shown me anything, it was how much more there was besides all this. Then the CEO's secretary walked in the room and shocked everyone with the announcement the meeting had been postponed until after lunch. I picked up my files and left the Conference Room.

Back in our offices, everyone was convinced there was trouble being covered up in the postponement. The entire department was buzzing with dire rumors. Later, we learned from our colleagues in other departments that during the investors' pre-meeting reunion there had been loud, hollering voices in French coming from the lounge room. They'd seen Monsieur Gerard of Club Méditerranée storm out of the room, practically running to the elevators. It couldn't look any worse, we all agreed.

Before lunch, though, our director called our team to his office and told us not to worry. "The contracts will be signed, I promise you that much," he assured us. "There are going to be some changes, but it's a done deal . . ." and so on.

It's funny how our biggest lies are the ones we tell ourselves.

That night I opened a bottle of Chardonnay when I got to my apartment. I changed into my hangout duds, went to the kitchen, made a cheese omelet, and settled on the sofa to eat it. At around seven, I left a message with Sylvia's answering service. Losing a client at any stage was always demoralizing for our department, but losing this one was particularly depressing for the entire firm. So why did I feel so relieved? Giddy, almost. Whatever it was that made it possible, Sylvia was at the heart of it.

The truth was I really wanted her to build her island paradise. I believed she would achieve something important with it. I wanted to believe she would.

We laughed like schoolgirls on the phone when I told her the resort would not be built. "Yes, cancelled, dead for the long foreseeable future."

"That's fantastic, Nancy. You did it. Darling, you're the best. But tell me, are they going to build elsewhere, can the cancellation be reversed?"

"Don't think so. One of the investors jumped ship. But, my, Sylvia, I'm surprised you didn't know that," I said, half teasingly.

"No, I didn't know," she said, her telephone voice lowering a few tones. "But I had you for that — didn't I? You were there for me. And I'm forever in your debt."

I blushed, I'm not sure why. "Us, girls got to stick to-gether."

"That is right." We laughed.

"So tell me, did the material I mailed you play any part in the outcome? Did it come in handy?"

I don't know what made me say, "Oh yeah. It was right at the top of the folders we gave out. They couldn't have missed it. It was a brilliant idea, Sylvia."

I didn't see Sylvia until ten months Later at Le Belvedere. It was late December, and I was on the yearly special Blue Ribbon New Year's plan, which meant we had the entire hotel to ourselves. The word among the girls was the work on Syl-via's island was going slow and that she wasn't around much. But she was there, at Le Belvedere, waiting to see me the day I arrived.

I pictured I'd find her wearing a hardhat, a pink one, but she was dressed as regal as always. We hugged in the lobby.

"So nice to see you." She confirmed how busy she'd been. "Yes, I've become unrecognizable." She laughed. "All work and too little play. But I'll always find time for you, darling."

She dismissed the Haitian man she'd come with and sat down with us in the garden of the hotel. Even the sand-walkers on the beach took a break when they saw our get-together. To the girls I hadn't met — there were several new faces — Sylvia introduced me as her favorite "founder."

Judging by how Sylvia was talking about it, her island project was now an open secret. "I've become a bore, I know," she was saying. "It's just been work, work, work, I'm sorry to say. But, ladies, Amazon Manor is coming!"

She tried to gloss over the troubles of her day to day, but she couldn't keep it to herself. She went right into it in detail. The nightmare it was trying to get anything done in Haiti, "I mean, you've got to see the boatful of bricks and stacks of lumber just sitting there for days;" and her frustration of having to deal with the arrogant architects, the boring engineers, and the lazy hardhats. "Men! It's unbelievable they're running the world."

The week moved on as expected. Sylvia only dropped by in the evenings. Nora told me she had spoken to Gabriella, who was unable to get away for the holidays. As for me, I reunited with the Boucher brothers, Charles and Guy, still wearing their matching net shirts. They seemed happy to see me. With them, I was finding out how reiteration and healthy competition bore its own delights. Then, on the eve of the New Year's party, we were treated to a surprise tour of Marinette Island, the name Sylvia had given her island.

In the morning mist Sylvia's motorboat, a former cruise ship tender, took us out into the choppy gray waters. For twenty minutes, we bobbed and listened to Sylvia's soprano swagger cutting over the boat motor noises. She stood on the bow steps, wearing a lifesaver under a yellow oilskin rain cape and a sou'wester.

"The actual existence of the Amazonian women may be a myth," she said, trying her sales pitch on us believers. "But here in the Kingdom of Marinette, my ladies, our vision of Amazonia will become reality, the seeds of a new order."

Our cheers made her smile as I'd never seen her smile. Her eyes twinkled with delight as she described "The amazing guests' suites and luxurious cabanas under construction as we speak — each with a Roman bath — were designed by none other than the Jacques Granges firm, the newest and hottest designers in Paris today . . ."

Through the open cabin door behind her, the deep greenness of Marinette Island appeared in the mist floating over the cloudy ocean. When Sylvia announced we were about to land, she signaled Nora and me to come forward. "I want you two to disembark with me," Sylvia said. "I want you two to be the first founders to set foot on my island."

I felt flattered, carried away by her gift of turning even something as mundane as getting off a boat into a historical event. After we landed, it didn't matter that I couldn't picture the paradise she'd been talking about among the chaos of construction materials and machinery strewn over a worksite as big as four football fields. That I couldn't see her world-conquering images on the rutted mud before me wasn't important. I realized what Sylvia dreamed of was not what drew me to her. Something else was sweeping me along, some phenomenon inside me with a hunger of its own.

Later that day I found Sylvia in the hotel garden, talking to a group of her minions. "Here, she is," she said when she saw me. She gestured at a chair next to her for me to sit and went on with her discourse, bracelets jingling with her every hand movement.

I looked around me at the smiling old faces at the table, stirring my rum special in a pineapple with the straws. Hearing their laughter reminded me of how I felt the first time I sat in Le Belvedere's garden and of all that had transpired since. And how the world hadn't come to an end, but spun anew. I felt as though some idea I once held deeply had been put to rest, expired in this sad, happy place. I couldn't tell what exactly, but it didn't matter. Its absence made me feel lighter, it had toughened me in some way. As the sun sank into the darkening sea, a light flickered across the water from Sylvia's island. I heard Sylvia inviting everyone to raise their glasses. I didn't catch what we were toasting this time. But that too didn't matter. I couldn't think of another place I would rather be.

# Dreaming in America

Mrs. Blanco has always known she had a smile, sensed it even before she became aware of it. When nothing else would do, her education, her figure, her presence, that simple pull at the ends of her lips spoke with a language of its own. This morning she knows she's going to need it. So sure she is, in fact, that after brushing she restrains from flashing her teeth at the mirror to preserve her smile's full strength.

Outside the window is dusky gray. She reaches for her floral dress, something to brighten up the Monday morning that awaits her. She closes the closet door softly, so as not to wake up her son who's still asleep in the bed they share. From on top of the night table, she picks up her reading glasses next to the *Selecciones del* Readers Digest magazine and slips them on. She wears them all the time now when it's dark.

The long hallways of the boarding house are gloomy silent, her roommates either asleep or gone to work. In the kitchen, she greets Rita, the owner of the *casa de bordantes*. No need to start shining her smile yet. The radio is buzzing the local Spanish news. Mrs. Blanco has her breakfast in between Rita's comments. They're mostly about the weather getting colder. Where Mrs. Blanco comes from *el tiempo* is not much of a subject. It's either raining or it isn't, and usually too hot. Not here, in the city of long coats. The first thing out of people's mouths here, friends or strangers alike, is the weather, how cold is it going to get or what's going to fall from the sky today.

Mrs. Blanco finishes putting on her face by the front door. She reaches into the bottommost of her purse for the keys and locks every lock before she steps away.

It all begins in the elevator, with the simple act of pressing the call button on the wall brass plate. The doors open on their own and she steps inside the mirror and metal box. Her belly shivers as the floor drops, a combination of dread and excitement she's still acquainting herself with since she arrived in New York. Part of the luxury trappings of a past future time, an aging modernity, she is only now catching up to.

For better or worse, everything is temporary. If she is certain of anything it's that. Exile with all its heartbreaks, the same as the guilty enjoyment of a New York elevator ride, is only provisional. The bearded atheists who had forced her and so many to flee her homeland would not keep her forever from the life God had meant her to live.

Outside, it's colder than it looks. She buttons up the winter coat Rita sold her for five dollars and tightens Amelia's red scarf around her neck. As she walks past the store windows in her stiff overcoat, her reflection isn't all that unappealing. It not only conceals her long-lost silhouette and keeps her warm; it also makes her feel part of the landscape, like another New Yorker.

At the bus stop, everyone climbs in one at a time, each dropping a token, unrushed. It is at moments like these too that she's reminded how far she is from home. Tokens instead of money, no one hustling to the empty seats, no conductor to collect the fare. The efficiency of it makes her wonder, though. In her town, buses had a driver and a conductor, and when they'd seen her a few times, she didn't need to signal her stop. Everyone was more in touch with each other, less orderly, sure, but more normal. She wonders how the *americanos*, as smart as they are, could have missed that, the simple human touch.

The downtown bus travels in the shade of Broadway's architecture, a sightseeing show for Mrs. Blanco — and the reason she preferred them to the subway. She presses her forehead on the icy glass window. She grins at the bright storefronts along the way, with their window displays projecting out to the street like movie screens with views of domestic scenes, gleaming kitchenware, and elegant mannequins wearing the latest styles. There's a kind of musical play choreography in the way New Yorkers march across the streets, in the stop-and-go of the vehicle traffic. The grandeur everywhere moves her, the polished sheen of rotating doorways, the assembly lines of yellow taxis, the sheer abundance of affluence. Her faith in the infinite might and wisdom of the *americanos* is reaffirmed at every intersection.

The bus stops at a red light.

When she left Havana, all she and her boy were allowed to bring was $120.00 and — as she liked to say — all the hope and Kleenex they could carry. And, of course, the fervent belief that the United States of America would never allow a Communist nation to take root just ninety miles from Key West. This wasn't only her opinion: everyone she knew was of the same mind. The end of the bearded revolutionaries was only a question of when — maybe a year at the most before she'd be back with her family around her again, back to where she was born and married and had her children, home until three weeks ago.

Today is a particularly difficult day for Mrs. Blanco. It's her first day out looking for a job, in search of employment, something she's never done or needed to do before. At forty-six, the only job she ever had was that of housewife and mother, work that had prepared her for just about anything except to look for employment — much less in a foreign land. The task does not intimidate her as much as the idea of having to ask for it in English, a language she loves to hear but she's incapable of articulating without embarrassing herself.

Mrs. Blanco looks at the note her exiled friend, Marta, had given her. "Get off on 34th Street. Walk to 8th Avenue, Garment Center. They're always hiring sewing machine operators in the factories around there," it says.

In Havana, she had a Singer machine with a wrought-iron foot pedal her husband bought her. She'd fashioned dresses and shirts for her children with it when they were younger, even sewn a camping tent for her son's Boy Scout troop once. Sew? Mrs. Blanco could sew just fine.

From the bus, she keeps watch of the street signs at every corner. "Get off when you see the Macy's store and walk around the area looking for Sewing Operator Wanted signs on building walls," Marta's note says.

Many things she never needed before or thought she ever would are needed now. Only a few weeks ago she still lived at home with her husband of twenty-two years and her two children. She'd known the comforts of a well-off existence, which had come with much struggle and only in recent times. But in less than a year of the communist takeover, it was all torn apart, beginning with the seizure of her husband's business, the family house, even the cars. Then came days of desperate rushing around like on a ship in the storm, throwing everything overboard, trying to sell, trade, and hide whatever remained of the family's assets. But the idea of seeking asylum didn't come until later when talk of an even more horrifying law was proposed. The enactment of what they called 'Patria Potestad.' The law that gave the communist government parental rights over un-emancipated children. Once the rumor took hold, the question of whether or not to leave the country was settled.

The communists could take everything she owns, she decided, but not her son.

Almost overnight, she found herself thousands of miles away, confined to a bedroom in an overcrowded boarding house in New York City with her twelve-year-old son, starting her temporary life of 'political' exile, a refugee — a 'worm,' how the *fidelístas* called the likes of her.

Although the hardships of her younger days now seem like something to look forward to, Mrs. Blanco doesn't allow herself to wallow in her misfortune as some of her fellow exiles do. Hope is fresh yet. Still, the day-to-day is far from easy. Rooming in an apartment full of political refugees is like living with a big wounded, grieving family. Rare is the night that she is not awakened by the muffled sobs of some of her roommates. Exile is the same as living in a permanent state of emergency, ever hanging to a single hope. Every rumor, every word printed or heard on the radio about the homeland has to be dissected, reinterpreted for hidden meanings, every piece of news a new topic to argue about. The one thing the entire exile commune agrees on, though, is, with God and the *americanos* on their side, everything the *comunistas* have stolen from them would be theirs again. And this was something Mrs. Blanco believes with all her heart.

Across the street, on the northbound side of Broadway, Mrs. Blanco notices a sign written in English and Spanish. It speaks of union, employment, and brotherhood. Compelled by a sudden impulse, Mrs. Blanco pulls the cord and gets off the bus, and then doubles back up the street.

The sweet smell of recently baked dough stops her on her tracks. She rests one hand on the shop window and stares at the trays full of happy-looking donuts arranged in rows. Mentally, she counts the change she has in her purse, hoping. But she knows all too well how much she has, or rather how much she doesn't have, then walks away thinking of all the weight she still could stand to lose — once again looking at the positive side so as not to weep.

She stands under the sign she saw from the bus and takes up the dark and narrow staircase. At the top landing, she halts by the opened smudged glass door. The stale air in the gray-walled office reeks of cigarette smoke and indifference. Facing a long counter dividing the room, a handful of people are lined up by a faded yellow line on the floor.

Mrs. Blanco steps in and surveys the women working behind the counter and at the desks beyond, pecking on their typewriters. A couple of suited men sit behind glass-partitioned cubicles.

She stands demurely at the end of the line and listens to the English-speaking voice of the bespectacled woman behind the counter, concentrates on it.

The person at the counter walks away and Mrs. Blanco moves up a step.

In front of her, there's a tall black lady and a Latina-looking one who's at the counter now. She's speaking to the bespectacled woman. The harder Mrs. Blanco listens to what they're saying the less she understands.

A minute later, she hears "Next." She remembers what next means. In English, every word sounds so much nicer to her, like in the subtitled movies, the voices of Doris Day, Elizabeth Taylor, and Audrey Hepburn, so musical even when uttered in anger. Yet she's just unable to articulate the words, as if her mouth isn't put together the same way as theirs.

The tall black lady steps up to the counter. Mrs. Blanco places the tip of her shoes on the yellow line on the floor. The tall lady seems upset. Something in the document the bespectacled woman handed her has set her off. Her voice is getting louder. She reminds her of those powerful-voiced Protestant preachers in the movies. Mrs. Blanco tries to decipher what each is saying. The noisier they get the less she comprehends them.

The tall woman starts to shake her finger at the impassive bespectacled face behind the counter. Suddenly she wheels and stomps away, hollering menacing at the entire place. When she reaches the door, she balls-up the insulting document, hurls it in the general direction of the wastebasket, and storms out the glass door.

Now the office staff is up, bunched in groups around their desks, ruffled by the irate lady. Mrs. Blanco is up next.

The bespectacled woman waves from the counter. "Come on up."

Mrs. Blanco approaches with a tentative smile: she didn't hear 'next.' Her throat tightens up. "Pleese, laydee, S-peak S-panish?"

The bespectacled woman turns around and with a cigarette between her fingers waves at someone and walks away.

Spanish Carmen comes to the counter: "How can I help you?"

Mrs. Blanco lets out a sigh of relief and broadens her smile. "Aaayy," she sings out. "Thank God you speak Spanish, *mi hijita*. What a relief."

Spanish Carmen almost smiles.

"Well, the truth is I am looking for work," she says leaning closer to the counter. "Let me explain: I have only been in this country for three weeks, yes. But I am a hardworking person and a fast learner, and I am willing to do whatever work that is being offered."

Carmen gives her a squint-eyed look. "OK, let's see your book."

"*Libro?*" Mrs. Blanco, unsure whether Carmen has understood, starts again. "Maybe I should tell you, I am a married woman. I have two children, yes, two. My oldest, my daughter, she's in Cuba with my husband, *los pobrecitos* ... I'm sure you must have heard how terrible things are over there now with those communists taking over, my God. But my son, he's with me. We had to bring him out right away before the communists start taking the children to Russia. Yes, that's another thing those communists are doing. But he's in school now, thank God. And God willing, my husband will be coming to join us very soon. Now, my daughter, we're not too worried about her. She's already eighteen and engaged, yes. She's going to marry a boy we know, a good boy. But in the meantime, well, my son and I have to stay here, you understand, until we can return. So you can imagine how difficult it's been for me to find a job without any English—"

"Excuse me a moment, Mrs. Blan-co, right?"

"Yes," she answers, reaching into her purse for her passport, her ID. "In Cuba, married women get to keep their maiden name, not like here. Yes, it is Blanco."

Carmen, assuming the walk-up is looking for her book, says as she flicks through the Rolodex, "Let's see . . . We have a few openings for iron operators today. Would that be something you'd want to do?"

"Ironing? Oh, sure. I can iron. My husband tells me no one, not even his mother, can iron his shirts as well as I do."

"All righty, then. Give me your book and I'll send you right out."

Mrs. Blanco hands her passport.

"Not this, your union book, or your card, whichever you brought with you."

"I am sorry *señorita*. I don't have a union book. I could get one if you tell me how—"

"Oh, oh. How can we send you out on a job, if you're not in our union? This is an employment office for our union members. This is not for anybody. I mean you have to be a member."

"No problem, I will join the union. Just tell me how."

"It's not like that. I'm sorry, the jobs we have are for our members in good standing only."

"This is no problem for me. No problem at all. I want to be a union member. Just tell me what I have to do and I will join your union. You see, we just arrived in New York and I need a job—"

"You've already told me, Mrs. Blanco. But I can't send you out unless you're in our union. It's just how it is."

"But I will be very happy to be a member of your union. What is it? Is there a fee?"

"Yes, well no, it's not just a fee. To join our union, you must first work in a union shop for at least three months before you can apply."

"You'll have to pardon me, Carmencita, *chica*. It's a beautiful name, Carmen. I almost named my daughter Carmen, yes. I have a cousin named Carmen too. She's my favorite cousin—"

"Mrs. Blanco…"

"Forgive me, Carmen, I will not bore you with it. But listen, if you give me the ironing job, I promise you I will come back in three months and ask for you personally and I will join your union. A promise is a promise."

Carmen looks over Mrs. Blanco's shoulders at the line. "Look, I'd love to help you—"

"But Carmen, my girl, how can I work for three months and then join the union if you don't give me the job first?"

"These are the rules. I'm really sorry."

"You mean you can't give me a job unless I already have a job?"

"Not really, but in your case, I'm afraid so."

"Why would I come to ask for employment if I am already employed? I'd be too busy at work!"

"I'm sorry. Take this brochure with you. Read it at your leisure. There's nothing else I can do. Next . . ."

Mrs. Blanco buttons up her coat. "Ay, Carmencita, really. I'm afraid it's going to take me a long time to understand this country." She straps her purse on her shoulder. "To have an employment office for people already employed—" She finished her comment with a silent headshake of disbelieve.

As Mrs. Blanco walks toward the glass door, the heat of emotion wells in her eyes. She halts next to the wastebasket. She looks down at the balled-up paper the screaming lady had shucked with such disdain. Quickly, she lowers herself, picks it up, slips it into her purse and walks out.

Two blocks away, she stops to decipher the words on the paper. It's a printed form filled out with ink but without a bearer's name on it.

"... *Jane Holly Blouses ... West 61ˢᵗ Street ... Steam iron operator ... Salary: $1.25 an hour ... attention: Mr. Weinstein.*"

Her face lights up. She has no reservations in applying for a job a disgruntled member of Carmen's union didn't want. Unions, what are they good for anyway? In Cuba, they called them *sindicatos,* like the one the communists first organized in her husband's factory and then abolished after they confiscated it. But if unions is how the Americans choose to call them, it is fine with her.

On Columbus Circle, Mrs. Blanco runs into a crowd of people waving signs of 'JFK for President.' She works her way around them and hurries down 60th Street, crosses West End Avenue, and turns on the corner. The Hudson River is just down the road.

A cold wind blows on her face, clean, crisp American air.

61st Street is solid with parked cars. She finds the address. A sign above the doorway says Jane Holly Blouses. She enters the building. Out of the biggest elevator she's ever seen, she encounters a pretty girl at the desk by the door. Mrs. Blanco switches on her smile and hands her the wrinkle-creased but now straightened flat employment form.

The receptionist, chewing gum, picks up a telephone, says one phrase and hangs up, then says something to her and points at a metallic door. The stained sign on it says 'Employees Only.'

"San-cue," Mrs. Blanco says.

She enters a high-ceiling workshop with long tables. Mr. Weinstein, a thirty-something, pleasant-looking man in a tie and dress shirt, comes walking from behind a stack of rolls of fabric. The out-turned toes of his shoes are shiny but dusty . . . a man who doesn't mind getting dirty at work. Mrs. Blanco approves.

She holds out the paper.

Mr. Weinstein doesn't look up at her smile. He scowls at the paper. "Where's your union booklet?"

She answers with her brightest smile something that sounds like this to Mr. Weinstein, "Chess, I lie to goo-erk bery mosh."

He releases a long sigh, steps back, and shouts over the machine noises "Josefina," then waits, glancing at Mrs. Blanco, sizing her up.

Spanish Josefina, short, with a round cheerful face, races over obviously pleased to be the boss's interpreter.

"Ask Mrs. Blanco if she has her union book or her ID card."

Josefina translates the question.

Mrs. Blanco takes a deep breath and is about to explain why she doesn't yet have a union card when Mr. Weinstein with the out-turned toes cuts her short. "Never mind," he says with a dual expression of pity and mirth on his pale face. "Tell Mrs. Blanco not to worry. Tell her to come back tomorrow at eight in the morning ready to start training. Ironing." He gestures as if waving an iron. "And tell her she'll be starting at a dollar an hour, not at a dollar twenty-five as it says in the form. OK?"

Then Mr. Weinstein adds without the need for translation, louder as if his Spanish would be better understood at a higher volume. "Ma-nya-nah worky on time. OK?"

The message is translated anyway and Mrs. Blanco, beaming, almost curtsies at her new boss. "San cue, bery bery mosh."

Walking back to the subway, Mrs. Blanco's eyes overflow with tears. She can't believe her luck. To have achieved what only twenty-four hours before seemed like a monumental impossibility feels nothing short of a miracle, as though the Virgin herself was watching over her.

Suddenly, she remembers how hungry she is and picks up her gait. Back in the rooming house, there are hot dogs and a can of Campbell soup waiting for her. Tonight, she announces to herself, she will take her son to the pizzeria on Broadway and celebrate. She slows her pace as she approaches a tumult in Columbus Square.

The crowd is so thick she can't see the end of it. Dozens of JFK for President cardboard signs are up all over the street and over people's heads. Motorcycle policemen are cutting off the traffic. Red lights are swirling. A sudden upsurge of voices and motor noises breaks out and she is dragged by the rushing human tide toward the edge of the sidewalk. A slow-moving black convertible as long as a yacht comes sailing slowly through the mass of bodies. And there, over the sea of outstretched fluttering hands, the figure of John F. Kennedy appears in a royal blue suit, his face under a crown of impeccable chestnut hair, and a smile of perfect white. Drawn by the delirious multitude, Mrs. Blanco reaches out to him as if attracted by an invisible magnet, and their skins clasp together for a magical instant. Then just as quickly, the candidate's caravan floats away.

Mrs. Blanco extricates herself from the mob. She walks away toward Broadway unaware of the importance she would later give to the event. A half-block up 61st Street, she begins to feel faint. She leans on a wall to wait for it to pass. Beside her, there's the tangle of tubes of a scaffold on the side of the building. On a tall windowsill behind her, she sees a neatly folded white paper bag. She takes it and peeks inside. There are two jelly donuts wrapped in wax paper, a capped coffee cup still hot, two sugar packets, a plastic stirrer and paper napkins. She looks around her at the busy sidewalk of incurious New Yorkers passing by. She sighs and puts it back, and walks away.

She halts abruptly, turns back, picks up the paper bag and rushes up the street with it.

On Broadway, she finds a bench in the median promenade. She sits down, pours the sugar into the steaming coffee, and stirs it. Slowly, she takes out a donut. Up by her lips, she breathes in its baked aroma and bites the sweet soft dough filled with even sweeter jelly as though performing a delicious but sinful act. Pigeons start gathering nearer. The November sun shines with a silver glow through the overcast Manhattan sky. She savors the donut unhurriedly until is gone except for the white sugary dust on her fingers. She looks into the paper bag, and summoning the phenomenal strength only motherhood could give her, Mrs. Blanco saves the remaining donut for her son.

She gathers herself up and takes the subway uptown.

In her room, she finds her son with his heavy white-sox feet resting on the radiator. He has the transistor radio up by his ear. She drops the groceries on the small table by the door and gives him a kiss on the cheek. He's busy mouthing along with the song playing, mimicking the singer. He's singing in English.

Mrs. Blanco doesn't fool herself thinking if she ever went out job-hunting again that she'd be hired the same morning, shake the hand of a presidential nominee, and find a bag with fresh donuts and coffee. But it had happened. And she had done it all on her own. She knew her exiled roommates were going to ask her how her day went, they always ask about everything. She'd have to be watchful of how she told it. Measure her elation, soften the magical aspect of it. Tragedies bring people together, but personal good fortune, not so much. To be an exile, to be forced to flee one's homeland and seek refuge in a foreign country, is no different than living with an open wound, hurting part of every moment.

Mrs. Blanco approaches her son. His head is bobbing in time with the music. She lets the sweet-smelling paper bag fall on his lap. He drops everything when he sees the donut.

"How did this get here in one piece?" he says, amazed.
"Son, you wouldn't believe the day I had even if I told you."
"Did you find anything?"
 Mrs. Blanco smiled.

# Up on the Roof

*Summer of '61*

The heat was so bad Jackie's handball felt like bubble gum when it bounced off the curb. An August heat wave had kicked in around noon and everyone on the block had taken off to the Amsterdam Avenue public swimming pool. And now Jackie was as bored as only a fifteen-year-old can get in the summertime. The gang never bothered to ask anymore the reason why Jackie always refused to go swimming with them. Everyone had a theory on it, and many of them had been discussed at some time or other, but no one could say why for certain or cared anymore.

Jackie pocketed the clammy ball and bopped across the way. A boy, a girl, it was hard to tell in those baggy chinos and over-sized T-shirt. 137th Street was deserted. All that came up from the Hudson River was a nasty breeze that blew on Jackie's face on crossing the street. She pushed the iron and glass doors into the lobby of 600. It smelled of stale cigarette smoke, fried food, and old people.

Jackie rode the clanking elevator up to the top floor and climbed the rest of the stairs to the roof.

The door swung out with a penetrating squeal and there was Birdman at his usual spot, his back to the empty pigeon coop, a cigarette dangling from his lips, unstirred by what would have been the natural response to see who had opened the loud, squeaky roof door.

"Hey, man, what's up?" Jackie stumped up the three wooden steps to the coop's platform.

Birdman's narrowed eyes smiled. "Hot enough for ya?"

"Freaking A." Jackie dropped down next to him. The pigeon dunk stink steaming out of the cage was so bad it amazed Jackie how Birdman put up with it. Jackie figured after so many summers minding those birds, his nose had probably burned from the fumes and he couldn't smell it anymore. For Jackie, this was part of what you had to bear with to spend some time with him. "Jesus, it's ten times hotter up here. How do you take it?"

Birdman shrugged one shoulder. "Got no choice. I've got to be here in case they come back early. Someone's got to lock up." He shot the kid an askance look. "Like it's news to you."

"You think the flock's gonna come back now with this roof hot like a furnace? It's like ninety-some freaking degrees. They're probably out in Central Park or something."

"They might come back early. You never know. Besides, they don't go off that far."

"How do you know where they go? They talk to you now?"

"The flock is getting old. That's how I know." Birdman glimpsed over his shoulder at Jackie. "Pigeons can't talk. But the aviary tells me a lot of things about them. I think you know what I'm talking about."

"I guess."

Birdman called his pigeon coop his aviary. It was no different from any you found on rooftops all over the West Side, handmade with discarded wood boards and cheap chicken wire, with a roof made of junked zinc sheets. What made Birdman's coop different was his devotion to it. The way he had built it up through the years, the pigeonholes and feeders he had added to it, and the hours he spent every spring repairing the damage the winter season left him. This year Birdman had painted the coop white because it was the only paint he could afford, and as he himself had forewarned, it now looked twice as dirty and stained than previous summers.

"How come you didn't bring the portable with you?" Birdman asked, popping open a can of Rheingold.

"The batteries are shot."

"Have you heard how the game is going?"

"Not today," the kid said. "But I got my money on Maris."

"Sheeesh, Jackie. You don't know what you're talking about."

"And you do?"

"Hell, yeah. Maris is just lucking-out. Mickey Mantle is the man. He'll beat Ruth's record and leave this guy so far behind, you won't hear from him again."

"Ah, Birdman, you ain't always right about these things."

"It's OK, Jackie. It doesn't matter to me much either way as long as the Yanks come out on top. That's all I care about. Hell, these players nowadays, they come and go. It's not like before. The Yankees, they're the only thing that matters. That won't change."

"Freaking A, Birdman. I've got no argument with you on that."

"I just like to know how the game is going, it's all," he said ruefully.

"I'll find out for you later. I'll go down and check on how it's going."

"Thanks, Jackie. I've got to wait here. You know, till they get back." He cocked his head at the kid. "And what's that I heard about you betting? Where did you get money, anyway?"

"Nah, I didn't make any bets," Jackie said. "I was just saying."

Jackie liked Birdman most because he was never surprised by anything. No matter how outrageous a tale he was told, what wonderful or horrible news he heard, he always listened to it as though he had known it all along. Like when Caryl Chessman was executed, he's reaction was "I knew the only way he was getting out of there was feet first." Even though his lawyer got a federal judge to issue another stay just one minute before they gassed him up. All 'cause the judge's secretary mis-dialed the number.

Birdman shuffled and shifted his weight around trying to find a more comfortable position on the narrow deck bordering the coop. Sometimes his languid gestures and quiet moans when he moved reminded Jackie of a wounded cowboy.

"Birdman, you still feeling bad about Palomo?"

"Sure. You've seen what happened to the flock since he didn't come back. Sure, I'm sore about it."

"How many females have you lost so far?"

"I stopped counting. About half of them are gone, I guess."

"Palomo was something else," the kid said. "A stud pigeon if there ever was one."

"Palomo was beautiful, yes sir. Remember last summer when he came back with five. Five females in one afternoon. Ever heard anything like it?"

"Yeah, I remember." Jackie thought about it. "Maybe the hens just gone out looking for him and got lost. Or somebody's snatched them."

"Got no way of knowing," Birdman siad. "It's not their fault. That's their nature. Females—" Birdman released a humorless chuckle and glanced over at the rubber ball bulging up in the side pocket of Jackie's chinos. "They'll fly off with any dominant male that coos them. It's how they are."

"So who do you got left?"

Birdman squinted his eyes at the kid. "You know who's left. You asked me about it yesterday and I told you. You know damn well who's left."

"Damn, Birdman, don't have to talk like that to me. I ain't supposed to remember everything you say."

"OK, Jackie, you're right. I shouldn't talk like that to you. Not to you."

Now Jackie stood up even more annoyed at his last remark and began pacing over the wooden platform, shoulders hunched, hands in pockets.

Birdman focused his cowboy eyes on the worn-out Keds with red laces stomping past him. "Hey, Jackie, I didn't mean it the way you think. OK? Sit down, will you? Here," he said, handing the kid his pack of Luckies. "You can have a smoke if you like."

"How many you've got left?" Jackie said, sitting down again.

"Don't matter, take it. Just don't get dizzy and want to puke again. Go slow this time. Don't puff so hard like you did. Just savor it, like."

"I got the hang of it. It only happened because I had a big lunch. I know how to smoke. It ain't like you need a high school diploma to smoke, Birdman."

"You calling me a dropout, there, kid?"

Jackie peered at the Birdman's expressionless face and laughed. "Come on, Birdman. What could they teach you in school you don't already know? I can't even imagine you in a classroom with them dungarees and those greasy biker boots."

Birdman chuckled. "I can't help it if you got no taste in dressing."

He flipped his cigarette butt and watched it fly over to the tar roof floor. Then he stretched his legs out in front of him, his black boots dull and heavy as he dragged them over the boards. Jackie often wondered what it would be like to have legs as long as Birdman's. Sometimes she wished she could be so no-sweat sexy like him, too.

The sun began to beat down on them and they moved to the shaded side of the pigeon-house. From this angle, they could see the Hudson River over the treetops on Riverside Drive and the New Jersey cliffs on the opposite shore. Across the roofs to their left, high above the massive dome of Grant's tomb, a solitary kite was flying high in the sky. Straight ahead, directly above the shimmering surface of the river was the Alcoa zipper sign with the moving words. On the clifftop stood the metallic structures of Palisades Amusement Park lit up in the sun.

"Ever been to Palisades?"

"Once," said the Birdman. "I'm not much for crossing over to Jersey."

"I dig going to Palisades," said Jackie, trying to hold back a cough. "The last time we went they had this show with a big orchestra and everything. It was great, man. The Coasters came out and sang. They were the coolest."

"Who's that, one of them new singing groups?"

"Jesus freaking Christ, Birdman. You don't know the Coasters? Where've you been, man?" Jackie jumped up and went into a spastic song and dance, head bobbing, fingers snapping, sneakers skidding on the wood planks. "Charlie Brown, he's a clown . . . Cool, Charlie Brown. . . ."

"Sit down, will yah," Birdman said, laughing. "You look like you're having a fit."

"Come on, man. Don't tell me you never called your English teacher Daddy-O."

"Sit down. You're making me nervous."

"Ah, Jesus, Birdman, you're such a square."

"I guess."

"Anyway, you're not supposed to like it. You're too old. What are you? You got to be like thirty," Jackie said, sweaty-faced from play-dancing and wincing at the idea of such advanced age.

Birdman took a long drag of his cigarette. "You think I'm thirty?"

"Well, are you?"

He grinned; it was more like a grimace. "Not yet, kid. Not yet."

They gazed out at the view in front of them. Jackie's round, soft face suddenly hardened with a thought.

"Birdman, do you think there's something wrong with me 'cause I don't want to go to the pool with the guys?"

He shook his head. "No."

"Birdman, why is it you never go out with girls?"

"I go out with girls."

"Never seen you with one."

"That's 'cause I haven't had a steady in a long time."

"You never talk about it any. Why don't you tell me about your girlfriends, Birdman?"

"Sheeesh," he hissed. "Like I'm going to talk about it with you."

"What's that supposed to mean?"

"Nothing. You out of your mind?"

"Why not?"

"Because you're a kid."

"You know," Jackie said. "I know why you don't want to talk about girls with me. I asked you, but I know what you think."

"So you do."

"Yes, I do." Jackie's shiny brown eyes were fixed on Birdman's face. "Damn right I do."

"What's eating you now, Jackie?"

"Nothing. Forget about it."

"All right then," Birdman said. "Tell me why don't you want to go to the pool with the guys?"

"For the same reason you don't want to tell me about your supposed girlfriends, I'd bet. Am I right?"

"Sure. Whatever you say, kid."

"Jesus, man. You're so weird sometimes."

"I'm weird all the time, Jackie."

"I'm leaving. This cage of yours is filthy. Look at my chinos—" Jackie said, cursing and spanking the seat of the trousers. "I'm splitting." Jackie started down the steps. "It's too freaking hot."

"You don't have to go," Birdman said, his eyes on the boats on the river.

"I got to go, anyway."

"Come back and tell me how the game's going, will you."

"If I get a chance," Jackie hollered back. The roof door squealed.

Jackie didn't come back that afternoon. Maris and Mantle batted two home runs each at Yankee Stadium and the Yanks came one game closer to winning the pennant. Before sunset, the flock returned to the coop. Without counting them, Birdman knew they were fewer than the ones he had let out in the morning. The females looked nervous and unhappy, and he wondered if he would ever have another male like Palomo.

He locked up the cage and threw the empty beer cans in the trash bin. Out of habit, he went over to the roof railing and leaned over it. He was six flights over the cobblestone, seven if you count the roof. Why not? he said to himself, looking down on 137th Street. I'm not going to kill myself over Palomo. I didn't do it over Patty O, or when I lost the Harley. Didn't do it over the dishonorable discharge, didn't do it when I should have. It wouldn't mean a thing now.

Down on the street, the boys from the block were back from the pool. They were all over the stoop of 601, towels around their necks, arms flying with teenage fire, talking about all the fun they had. While Jackie stood to one side leaning on the rail, the lone girl in the bunch, as always. Birdman had known for a long time why Jackie refused to go to the pool with the boys. It was easy to understand, he thought. In spite of all she tried, she knew the boys would never accept her as one of them or ever would. She was a girl and they were boys in the heat of adolescence, what else was there to say? Still, Birdman felt sorry for her, for having that problem. He had learned a lot from her since she started coming to see the pigeons. She understood his loneliness as he did hers, without having to talk about it. Today's little episode was a fluke and nothing to worry about, he thought. The heat was to blame.

Now Jackie was alone on the stoop. She was bouncing her handball against the sidewalk with bored swings of her arm. The sun was beginning to set and the Sunday strollers were coming out of the buildings. She slipped the ball in her pocket and waved up at the Birdman leaning on the roof railing. He waved back and she went inside.

# The Numbers Vendor

When Nelson *el Raro* walked out of his house the morning heat had settled on the cobblestone. Breakfast was sitting nicely in his belly now and his second day without sleep was but a faint unpleasantness under his skin. Most of all, he felt lucky today, an altogether unfamiliar sensation for him.

Down by the bay, the Emboque plaza and the launch docks were bustling with people and buses in the warming sun. Even the sky above it was full of activity with red-and-yellow kites swooping in the saline breeze and all the birdlife over the harbor—the loud screeching gulls, the fast-moving sparrows, the high-hovering buzzards with their long wings flat and still up near the clouds.

He stopped a moment to watch a *frutero* building a pyramid of oranges on his cart, while he listened to the other vendors hawking their goods for the people coming and going on and off the harbor launches. Each vendor had his own distinctive personal rhyme. His favorites were those of the *tamalero* and the peanut vendor because theirs were the most musical. Nelson would always know precisely what others meant when speaking of their hometown, their homeland, by simply focusing his thoughts on El Emboque docks on a windswept morning like this one.

He browsed his way through the hectic plaza to see Cheo Calandro, the old blind man who had been selling lottery bills at the same spot ever since he could remember. He thought the ancient numbers vendor had a soft spot for him because whenever he stopped by for a casual greeting, Cheo Calandro would become very talkative and engage him in long, preposterous conversations on subjects that, although interesting, he could not take seriously coming from an illiterate son of African slaves.

But Cheo Calandro was not just anybody. He was considered one of the town's landmarks, worshipped by many because of the countless winning lottery bills he'd sold to people who became rich overnight with the prizes. And yet, despite all the good fortune his lottery bills had brought to so many, the old man was back there every day, sitting with his colorful rack of bills at his side in his nook in the rocky wall where the church stands.

As Nelson left the plaza behind, he decided that if the old lottery vendor sold him the winning number, he would give him half the prize.

"Good morning."

Cheo Calandro was sitting on a wooden Coca-Cola crate, his brown, sinewy forearms resting on his knees. "Who's there?" he asked, straightening up his back.

"Nelson Vargas. Remember me?"

The blind man's cloudy eyes wandered. "Ah yes. You are the son of Raul *El Bolitero*. How is he these days?"

"Good. Working," said Nelson unnecessarily loud.

"¡*Muchacho*!" the blind man let out, covering one ear. "I'm blind, not deaf."

His eyes again moved awkwardly. "Tell me one thing: are you anything like your father? I ask because your father told me he doesn't believe in luck anymore. How am I going to make a living if people stop believing in luck?"

"That's a good question. But I've come to take a chance on the thirteen," Nelson said, studying the green-printed lottery bills on the rack, pinned side by side like on a clothesline.

"You?" The blind man nodded his head in approval.

"Yes, well, today is the thirteen of March," Nelson told him. "I've decided to make it my lucky number from now on. I know people think it's an unlucky number but—" he shrugged, his body language wasted on the blind man. "I've got my reasons."

"Well that is a very important decision you have made," Cheo Calandro said with a grave scowl. "Not a trivial thing like people say."

"No, of course not," Nelson said, humoring the man. He pulled his wallet out of his pocket.

"The thirteen, huh?" Cheo Calandro scratched his hairless, sweaty head. "You do know this number is very popular among my regular buyers, don't you?"

"Truly?" Nelson said curiously surprised. He looked at the three pesos in his wallet.

"Oh yes. But you know what?" Cheo Calandro said. "After a lifetime of selling lottery bills, I know this much: this numeral is not a lucky one by itself."

"What? Do I have to buy something else with it?"

The blind man slapped his thigh, laughing. "No, nothing like that."

"I don't get it."

"It's simple, *chico*. The numeral thirteen, on its own, brings luck to no one."

The blind man waited for Nelson to say something; when he didn't, he went on. "That is unless that someone is naturally akin to its influence. You must be the type of person it likes—if you know what I mean. Then and only then will this number bring in the goods. The thirteen has to choose you. It's not enough for you to choose it."

The blind man paused with a mischievous grin on his thick lips. "But you probably think this is all nonsense."

"No, no, I'm listening," answered Nelson with a superior smile. How could he begin to explain to the lottery vendor of all he already knew about numbers, or of the many hours he had spent alone in the university's library while the riotous demonstrations were taking place outside, hiding in the section for the Occult Sciences with those forbidden volumes of ancient secrets all to himself? What could this old man know of Ramon Llul and the endless combinations that can measure the cosmos . . . ? When out of nowhere, as if for the sole purpose of shattering his mental self-assertions, eight carefree seagulls swooped down over his head and alighted on the wooden frame of the lottery display rack, each flying down and landing with such an uncanny precision and grace that it left Nelson feeling an itchiness in the pit of his stomach.

He informed the blind man of the gulls on his rack, but Cheo Calandro discarded it with a nod of his head. "They're new around here," he said, half-covering his mouth so as not to be overheard. "They come around when I talk about these things. They only want to see if I really know what I'm talking about."

The blind man had to cover his whole mouth not to giggle aloud. When he got over it, he raised his brown head and looked at Nelson as if making eye contact. "The truth is that all numbers are of good fortune. Some obviously more than others. But that is simply because people make them that way."

"I don't understand," Nelson said. More gulls were landing on the lottery display and the floor of the niche. The ones already by their feet were walking around as if someone were feeding them. It occurred to Nelson that perhaps the blind man was in the habit of feeding the birds around this time. Why else would these wild dockside gulls be behaving like this?

"How could that be?" Nelson said.

"Simple," the blind man replied as if very glad to have been asked. "All things are affected by the pull of people's fixation on them. For example, the numeral thirteen is recognized throughout most of the world as an unlucky number, as you have well said." Cheo Calandro let out a grunt intended to mean, Who knows why? "Personally," he said. "I don't see anything wrong with it. But right or wrong, mistakenly or not, it's been fixed on people's minds that way and this causes a big pull. The result is clear: an endless set of repercussions, an unlimited chain of effects affecting the numerology in all living things and material things. Curiously enough, it's not the same with inorganic beings. They're another story."

Nelson was too distracted to listen. A flock of seagulls was now all over the niche's floor, and he could have sworn they were indeed listening to the blind man.

"What I've noticed about the thirteen," Cheo Calandro went on, "is that it is a most faithful numeral. The more you conduct your life within its domain, the more your luck increases. In this aspect, it's no accident this number is the favorite of so many people. It can be generous to a fault."

Cheo Calandro drew a long breath. "The truth is I've caught myself wondering about these things once or twice before, but it's a waste of time."

"Why is that?"

"Because I am no good for the thirteen. And I've got a sneaking suspicion this number is not good for you either. Something tells me you should not interest yourself with it too much."

"Does that mean you're not going to sell it to me?"

"No, that's not what I mean," the lottery vendor responded, shocked. "Clearly I would sell you this bill with pleasure. Who am I to make such a decision for you? The problem is I'm all sold out."

Cheo Calandro burst out laughing with the abandon only a blind man can.

Spooked by the man's laughter, Nelson pocketed his wallet and took off across the sun-beaten plaza. The itchiness in his stomach had turned into a painful fluttering, which for some reason he thought he could soothe with cold coconut water.

The vendor fished a coconut out of the iced water in a cut-off oil drum, chopped the top off with a machete, inserted a straw into the opening and handed it to Nelson. It cost five cents.

Nelson leaned on one of El Emboque's pillars in the shade and sipped the coconut water. He peered at Cheo Calandro on the other side of the steaming plaza. A woman with a black veil over her head was inspecting the lottery bills on the old man's rack now, but not one gull was anywhere to be seen. They must have flown away while he was looking away, all thirty or forty of them. Hard to believe, he thought, though not impossible if you'd seen their choreographed aeronautics.

Nelson threw the empty shell on the pile. The hot midday sky was as still as a picture now, nothing moving in it but the rising black smoke from the departing number 6 bus he'd just missed. He headed into the docks instead and hopped on the next ferry launch across the harbor. In Havana, he was bound to find a vendor with his number. If he was lucky.

# Gloria

Cupid's bow-shaped lips and even teeth of pure white gave him the perfect smile. And he knew it. It was obvious. Why else would he go around smiling at everyone like a priest at mass sprinkling holy water on his flock, pulling out his lips at teachers, male, female, young and old, at the other kids, boys and girls, at the school bullies even, at the bifocal geeks for god's sake, at anyone of any race, color, or creed? From the lowliest to the mightiest, no one escaped his tall lighthouse-beaming face, not even me, although I hated it when I became his target, precisely because he smiled at anybody and I didn't want to be just anybody—not to him. If he caught you looking, he might grant you one of his winner's smiles as a sort of handout, you know, his perk for having crossed the threshold into his enchanted web, and Oh, how I hated him when he did that to me. Or when he and I happened to cross paths in the hallways, between classes, or on the street going to and fro, and he'd flash those grinning lips in my direction without giving me enough time to turn away before my face started to flush as if a sudden heatwave had rushed into it, boy, those were the times when I hated him most, hated him to death.

At some point, I forget when, I devised a defense mechanism to avoid falling prey to those weaponized smiles of his.

My plan: to look him in the eyes instead, fix my four-eyed glance strictly into his, focus only into those glassy brown or amber crystal marballs of his while keeping clear off his lip sorcery. But what a mistake that was. My retaliatory scheme crumbled as soon as I let my guard down, or accidentally dropped my gaze. I understood then that whatever his smile did to me, whatever it was that set off that hot spell in me which brought me to the edge of dizziness every time, was no match to his supermanish eye-to-eye X-ray glances. I hadn't count on those prismatic eyeballs of his going right through me like they did. Peeling me like an onion of every layer of my defenses, tearing through my fake smugness down to that gooey lava matter cooking my insides . . . God, the way he could undress me with one up-and-down, rip off my blouse and jeans, leave me in the raw without blinking . . . God, I hated him so I wanted to hurt him, physically harm him, punch him, slap that face of his, scratch his eyes out . . . But the same as when you see a nasty car accident or a sweet-faced baby in a carriage, or somebody running naked, I couldn't avert my eyes from his, ever, as if he owned me. My pathetic 'iron will' was nothing against the draw of the rare earth magnet of his presence . . . sometimes in my bravest moments, it felt good just to bump into him without acknowledging his existence, you know, for the petty satisfaction of being able to pretend to ignore him, which made me feel really, really good, like picking a bloody crust with my nail . . . those nights I would fall asleep to the sweetness of my hate and sleep so well. Sick? Maybe. But hey . . .

Then came that day. Had I'd been waiting for it? Sure, I had. Hoped for it. Daydreamed about it. Except I just couldn't imagine how it would come about, if ever. After school, crossing Amsterdam Avenue, I looked over my shoulder and there he was, alone, all six feet of him, his battered schoolbooks swinging in one hand. Oh, yeah, his smarmy smile across his face, his disposable version—I recognized his repertoire—a hanging slight grin of self-involvement on his upturned upper lip under his Roman nose under his arching eyebrows, like two brown umbrellas over his amber eye and his other eye (yes, his other eye was hazel, weird, right?) The one he squinted at the world beyond his universe with its flowing and ebbing effect, calling me and dismissing me at the same time. Hi, he said. Hi? To me? I said Hi, so cool I was. His lips contracted and his smile disappeared. No teeth to be seen. I couldn't remember ever seeing his unsmiling face. I thought I would die. Then he said, "See yah," and bopped away, his back to me, chanting a song that spells my name, G-l-o-r-i-a.

He knew my name? That night in bed I felt my insides melting like an iceberg drifting into equatorial waters, lique-fying what I'd known as hate into a warm viscous fluid thicker than blood, slumbering into open-eyed dreams. Love. It was love.

When I heard of his motorcycle accident, I didn't cry. How could I cry over something I couldn't believe possible? Even after I stood among the crowd huddling around his closed casket, I couldn't do it. Later at his burial, listening to the sobbing of dozens of my schoolmates in their Gothic black, I stared at the polished casket shining in the hot, bright summer sun, slowly descending into the ground past the As-troturf carpet framing the hole, flowers raining on it, I didn't believe it. Even as I let go of my long-stemmed white rose when the coffin hit the soft dirt bottom, I refused to believe it. How could someone so alive be dead? How could such a burning feeling have no living source? No one except him had known how I felt about him. My beautiful hatred, the asthmatic excitement that had haunted me so, kept me up through long sweet sleepless hours, filling me with the most delicious fantasies that spoke to me in the secret language of his lips, and the sky-parting metamorphosis he caused when he sang my name. Gone? No. Never.

# Papa's Bastard Son

Sometimes you look at the world and you can't understand it for all you try. They tell you the trick is to adapt, to get used to it, to conform. I know that much already. What other choice is there? Well, sure, there is something else you can do but you don't do it because, first of all, you're not that crazy. You have your health, your desires, your ambitions; you are made for living. It's what you do. And dying, death, going down with the ship might be all that they say it is but I am not built for it. I will not argue about it, either. I have friends who love talking about it. Not me. You want to die? You go ahead. Leave me out of it. What's the hurry? It's not just the dying. It's all the time they expect you to stay dead.

This is why I will not go out there in an inner tube like those lunatics did. I'd rather wait for the right moment, the right tide. I am tired of arguments, opinions, debates. Talk, talk, talk, a black-market of endless verbalizing. I want work that I can do with my hands, in silence. I want to make things, useful things. I want to go to work, come home, pay the rent, eat, make love and go to bed. At least I'd like to try it for a while. Maybe it's not for me. Maybe it's too late for me. But as I sit here covered in dust and sweat, watching the sea turn from emerald to lead, I wish I could float away like a paper boat on a flooded gutter after a downpour. Float out of sight into that liquid desert and wake up in the world, in the real world. The one you see on television, in the movies, the world of those people who look at us and smile those strange smiles. People of the real world. True, sometimes I don't understand them, but I think that comprehension is overrated anyhow.

I have a friend who says, "Roberto sleeps on the beach on Sundays because he thinks a bunch of mermaids is going to pop out of the water and carry him to Key West." What he really means is I sit here on these night sands waiting for some benevolent rafter to ask me to join them. "*Está loco*," they say. But I don't argue anymore. Mermaids . . . I wouldn't even know how to make love to one.

Who's not a little loco on this never-never island, anyway? This water-locked madhouse where nobody calls anything by its real name, unless you're talking to a foreigner, or to your saints. I used to tell my friend, "You're mistaken. I don't spend the night on the beach waiting for some imaginary rafter to give me a ride to freedom. Aren't we supposed to be freer than anyone has ever been?" But I don't argue anymore. What for? But—just between you and me—it got me thinking. Sometimes I think that is exactly what I come here to do.

Like a child with a wet bottom, playing with a toy shovel night after night, hoping for a ghost rafter to take me away.

Granted, I've been accused of being a dreamer. But I have my moments of lucidity too. I've been known to wade waist-deep in the heavy waters of reason and see things and faces for what they really are. If not, then why would I be sitting here breathing that dead fish smell and watching the sea stir like boiling crab soup in front of my starving eyes? I do not long for freedom, maybe just a better prison.

I don't mind confinement. What's so bad about having a cell of your own? How much space or things does a dreamer need? Look at me. I wouldn't take too much space in any raft. Hey, brother, just give me a little corner there out of everybody's way. Nobody will even notice me. Freedom, what is it anyway? I'm not sure I'd recognize it even if it slapped me across the face . . . Until we hit land, that is.

Land!

The real world. The New World. The world of my forefathers. At least half of my genes, the white ones, originated there. Well, maybe in Europe but by way of El Norte like the charros call it or Yankeelandia as the gallegos say. Call it what you will, half of me belongs there. Still, they keep saying the same things about me. "Leave Roberto alone, the poor man has gone loco. Thinks he's half-American." But, as I've said, I don't argue anymore. I have the two things I need to prove them wrong. One is inside me: my indisputable certificate of authenticity. The other is inside the wall of my bedroom—my mother's bedroom before she died.

When I think of her, the surf, the sound it makes becomes a form of silence. And the moon . . . Where is it? It's gone out of sight again, taken the light of the world with it.

Moon-face. That was what my mother used to call me. "God," she would lament between peals of laughter. "You don't look a thing like your Papa." But it doesn't matter, the looks, I mean. I have the DNA and the manuscript. My DNA will prove what the manuscript cannot and vice versa. You say I don't look anything like my Papa? OK, check my DNA. You say, OK, my DNA confirms the bloodline and such, but it's of no consequence because I was born out of wedlock, an illegitimate child, a quickie in the shed, an unlucky bastard. OK. This is when I will swagger forward and pull out the envelope and slip the script out like a gunslinger draws his six-shooter, and say, "Here, feast your eyes." And I will unveil the manuscript — Papa's autobiography, a work no one knew it existed — and they would fall on their asses in absolute awe.

"Could it be the real thing? It looks real enough . . ."

Sure, they will rush it to the experts. Only to find out the truth. And I'll become an instant celebrity, rich, privileged. Then, when I get tired of all the attention, I will move to a farm and spend the rest of my days as Papa did in Ketchum, far from the sea, where I can work with my hands and create things. Things that no one needs but maybe some people might find useful, as with Papa's work.

Why Papa ended it the way he did, I'll never understand. No one called him loco when he stuck that double barrel in his mouth and blew his head off. That head so loaded with wonder and prose, so ripe for the picking, all the knowledge and insight it contained splattered all over the wall.

The pain, they say, the pain was too much. In his case, it was the sane thing to do. Me, they called loco when I tried it. It wouldn't be the same with me. Even with his genes swimming within me, it wouldn't be the same. Those certifiable genes he passed on to me by way of a sixteen-year-old mulatica who became the co-author of me do not make it the same thing. Why? I'm not sure. But as you know by now, I don't argue anymore. What's the use?

Sure, you might have his genetic matter and his pen — oh yes I have his pen. His famed fountain pen, a Parker 61 prototype with stainless steel cap and gold-filled trimming, a beauty. The one he used on who knows how many historic literary documents. Except it has no ink. Can't get ink for it anywhere. They refuse to give me any because they say I'll drink it down. I only did it as a joke, a juvenile prank. Twenty years later, I'm still without it. Yes, I do have his pen. But it's dry, dry like this island.

I would never forget that day mother pulled me aside and said with an air of nostalgia and wonderment but not of love, "This here pen belonged to your Papa. He gave it to me the day he gave me the manila envelope with the papers and said to me with his bad yanki accent, 'Mirta, I want you to have this. You may not think it's much now, but you wait a few years and see.' He was right. To me, it was just a pen and a pile of papers." Then she let out one of her African laughs of joy and pain. "How was I to know those papers contained his most secret secrets? One of humanity's greatest literary treasures. I was only a stupid girl then. You were still in my belly, smaller than a mouse. Then he disappeared forever aboard his Pilar, sailed away into literary martyrdom. All he left me was you and those yellow, dog-eared pages. Better than nothing, no?"

A pale light spreads over the beach like silver dust. It is in that strange moonlit instant that I first see her coming. Her boyish body and Olympian long and lean legs striding toward me out of the foaming surf.

She is gorgeous, a miracle bathed in moonlight. She sits beside me on the sand, her casual, languid movements in rhythm with the breaking waves. I take a good look at her long legs to make sure they are not covered with green scales. No, this one is no mermaid. She's all caramelized flesh and blood.

"You are Roberto el Loco, no?"

"Roberto, yes. Loco, I'm not so sure—"

"Well, whatever, my cousin Chicho told me to come and ask you—you know Chicho, no?"

I nod yes.

"Anyway, he told to me to tell you that the raft he was building is finished and he's ready to push it out," she says, pointing at the other end of the beach. "So he sent me over to offer you a place on it if you want it." Her singsong voice is sweet, nothing like her Amazonian physique.

I laugh. "Yes, yes, of course. When are we sailing?"

"Look, cousin Chicho says the raft fits eight people. And he told me to tell you there's space for one more if you want to come."

"Is this a joke?"

She snaps her lips in that sassy way only habaneras can. "*Coño, chico*, do I look like I'm joking?"

No, she didn't. Still. "Why me?"

"Look, man, I'm just here to give you this message. You can come or you can stay. But you've got to decide now. They're getting the raft ready, *ya*," she says, looking away

"Where exactly?"

"Over there." She extends her arm and points at a single light at the end of the curved shoreline. "Near the fish plant."

I had to laugh again. "Come on, what's this all about, really? Your cousin and I don't even know each other that well."

"Everybody knows you on this beach. Everyone knows you've been wanting to escape for months—"

"For years," I correct her.

"Whatever." She starts to get up as if she's already done her duty and now cares little whether I come or not. "Well?"

I look up at her statuesque silhouette towering over me. Was this my ride to freedom? "Is this for real?"

She gives me a sideways look. "It's now or never."

I hesitate a few seconds too much. "*Mira, chico*, so what's it going to be? You've got to tell me now. Plenty of others are dying for that space on the raft."

The realization shot like a heatwave through my veins. I jumped to my feet. "OK, OK, but first I have to go home and get some things, you know, my documents . . ."

"Wait. There's no space for bags or anything. You can bring your documents and whatever in a plastic bag and the clothes on your back, but that's it. Not a thing more: Chicho's orders."

What would it all mean without Papa's manuscript? "Yes, yes, of course," I said, knowing I wasn't going anywhere without it. "Just let me run home a moment and be right back. OK?"

"How long will you be?"

"Sing a song and I'll be here by the time you're finished. Don't you move. Wait for me . . ."

I took off running, her voice behind me like a mermaid's song telling me to hurry. I couldn't believe it. I ran as fast as my feet could go over powdery sand, transported by the magical quality of the moment.

A minute later, I'm at my door. My home of a lifetime, a two-story beach house my abuelo had built with his lottery prize in Santa María del Mar before the Revolution, of which I was only allowed to occupy two rooms on the second floor.

I fly up the cold granite stairway. The other three families in the house are asleep. I tiptoe into the kitchen, pick up the crowbar and head to my bedroom—mother's old bedroom. I stand before the wall that contains the family treasure. I remove the ancient mirror with the baroque gilded frame. My heart is racing. With the crowbar, I start poking into the plaster around the nail where the mirror had been hanging, the X spot.

I try very hard to keep it as quiet as possible. But how do you open a hole in a brick wall quietly in the middle of the night? I placed a bedspread on the floor but the ancient brick and plaster crumbles down loud anyhow. Sweat is dripping down the side of my dusty face. My hands start to burn and tremble. I can't believe what is happening or what I'm doing. Some part of me is already looking back at this moment as though it happened long ago.

For the first time in my life I am going to hold the manuscript in my hands, actually see the family treasure, three decades after my mother left it concealed in the hollow of the wall awaiting this moment. The idea of it is even more incredible to me than Chicho's offer of freedom. Liberty or death, I say mockingly to myself as I pound harder on the wall.

Suddenly, I hear shouting in between swings and hits.

"Hey! What the hell you're doing up there, Roberto?" The voice feels like iced water down my back. "It's two o'clock in the damn *madrugada*. Some of us got to go to work in a few hours, cojones!"

It's my downstairs neighbor, a paladar owner—the last guy who wants the law coming anywhere near here these days. I keep swinging the crowbar, going as fast as I can.

"Roberto! *Loco de mierda*." Now it's the upstairs neighbor, the Committee Delegate, doing the yelling. "This is insupportable." I hear his wife joining in. "I'm calling the police. Oh yes, this time I am . . . I've had enough of that lunatic."

I'm tearing into the wall like a gold miner swinging his pickaxe into a newfound gold streak. I know the manuscript has to be in there. Mother would not lie to me. "The family treasure, son. The master's last words. Your Papa's gift to us." My ticket to paradise.

My arms and my face are covered with plaster dust. I taste it on my lips. Where is the damn manuscript? I can already see through into the next room. Where is it? Mother, you told me it was here. Dig right behind the mirror, it's what you told me. Start where the nail is.

The shouting starts to multiply throughout the house, louder and angrier, like a gathering lynching mob. "Roberto! You crazy maniac. I'm going up there and kick your ass, I swear. Stop that banging already . . . Yes, Robertico, *por favor* . . . I will call the police this time, I'm warning you."

Almost half the wall is gone but I can't stop now. Mother, where is it? My fingers are bleeding . . . Wait. What is that? I hear a series of hard blows that shake up the house to its foundations. It isn't my hammering. I hear it again. It's my door coming off the hinges.

"Roberto, *hijo de puta* . . . the police are here . . . you son of a bitch." The doorframe cracks and splinters off the frame.

I keep pounding on the wall with all my might. Then, through the dusty brown light of the ceiling lamp, I notice something wrapped in green canvas. Is that it? Is it? It's the manuscript rolled up inside a piece of olive green tarpaulin. I reach for it—

It is here when I feel a flash of lightning, like a streak of moonlight rippling on choppy waters; it always comes at this exact moment. It never ceases to take me by surprise despite the countless of times it has happened before, a lightning across a starry night. And again, I savor the blood, the plaster on my lips, and the all-consuming numbness sets in. It starts in my legs and works its slow death up my body until my life ends again.

And again, it is midnight. And I am sitting on the night sands under the same battered moon over the same ocean of ink. The same sweat-soaked Saint Augustine emptying the ocean into a hole in the sand, pretending to grasp the incomprehensible, waiting for the future to let me in.

# The White Wingless Angel
# of Dove Key

*a novella*

## ONE

*What did I remember? I remembered water, animal water, burning into my eyes and nose. I remember it tossing and hurling me out of roaring surges, swallowing me into its darkest depth, all the horrors of life compressed into a single moment. And then the soundless crash of the pitch-black, silent nothingness of everything ceasing to exist, but for a faraway rippling in the center of my being wanting it all to be as before.*

The fishermen who found him among the mangroves in Dove Key could hardly believe his blanched naked body, nipped by fish and crabs, could still produce a heartbeat. They motored him to the Tavernier landing where the local deputy loaded his breathing cadaver on a pickup truck and drove northbound on the sun-beaten pavement of US 1.

Minutes later, the red pickup pulled in front of a low flat-roofed building with the words 'FLA KEYS CLINIC INC.' stenciled on its bleached façade. Nurse Parker, wearing a white-winged cap and a lab coat over T-shirt and jeans, stepped out into the noon glare. Luther, a corpulent dark-skinned man, the clinic's orderly and janitor, followed her out.

"Got here fast as I could," the deputy said, his broad red face in the shade of his visored cap, his thumbs under his service belt. "He looks dead but he's still breathing."

Nurse Parker took a sun-squinted look at the truck's flatbed. In between two sooty tires, she saw the mud-smeared soles and the dirty blonde head speckled with seaweed of a body rolled up in a straw mat. "Why did you bring him here?" she said. "You should've taken him straight to a hospital."

"Didn't know what else to do. Dr. Levin's hospital still under construction," the deputy said, removing his cap to wipe the sweat of his brow. He knew Dr. Cohn's private clinic was primarily set up for the care of outpatients, unequipped to handle critical emergencies—but it was a short ride from his home. "I figured it'd be okay."

Luther spoke up, "There ain't nobody here today but Miss Parker—"

"It's all right," she said, signaling at both men. "Bring him around back. Let's clean him up."

The deputy huffed his end of the stretcher. "Where's Dr. Cohn today? Playing golf?"

Nurse Parker gave the deputy a sideways look. "In Miami with Dorothy. Don't worry, I'll tell him who brought in the patient."

In the rear of the building, they lay the body on a canvas cot and unrolled the mat in which the fishermen had wrapped the body. Luther hosed it down as Nurse Parker indicated. A rainbow formed in the sunlit water splashing off his skin. Nurse Parker felt the multihued mist on her face. "Not so hard, Luther. This isn't a cah wash."

"Yes, mam," he said, smiling at that accent of hers.

As the swamp sludge spilled off limbs and torso onto the cement floor, the chiseled physiognomy of a most handsome young man began to appear from under it. The deputy, Nurse Parker, and Luther stood in silent contemplation over the body. Its wet glistening skin shone whiter than the nurse's lab coat. A body that by all appearances should be dead but was not.

Nurse Parker leaned over almost nose to nose with her patient. "He is breathing."

"Told you," the deputy said.

"OK, bring him in," she said. "Be careful."

In the hothouse heat inside the consultation room, the deputy and the orderly laid the body on the examination table. Luther flipped a switch and the window air-conditioner clanked on. Nurse Parker turned on the bright overhead lamps.

"Is he going to make it?" the deputy asked.

"At this point, Ray, your guess is as good as anybody's. Tell me what happened to him."

The deputy told her what he said he knew.

Nurse Parker lifted the patient's eyelids with her thumb. His blue irises and red smudged white of the sclera made her grimace with pity. "Did anybody try to pump him for saltwater and gave him mouth to mouth?"

The deputy shrugged. "Maybe the fishermen did."

Nurse Parker unpinned her nurse's cap from her gray-streaked blonde bun. She washed her hands in the sink and proceeded to check the patient's vitals and sterilize his lesions. The deputy pulled out a notepad and a ballpoint pen from the pocket behind his badge. "How old you think he is? Hard to tell laying there like a statue."

"He looks no more than eighteen to me," Luther said. "What'd you reckon, Miss Parker?"

Nurse Parker had the stethoscope plugs in her ears. "My god," she said. The boy's skin was colder than the metal end of the scope. "His heart rate is 26 slash-zero—unreadable. It's got to be wrong." She glanced at Luther and pointed at the jar with the tongue depressors. He handed her one. Holding the patient's chin down, she inserted the wooden stick in his mouth and peered inside beyond his perfect teeth, then threw the stick in a pan.

"Well?" the deputy said.

"Hard tellin' not knowin'."

"She ain't done yet," Luther translated.

Nurse Parker walked to the white cabinet and came back with an ear dropper.

Puzzled, the men watched her fill the dropper with dis-tilled water. Back by the examination table, she turned the boy's head to one side and emptied the liquid in his ear—a trick she'd read about in a medical journal that could bring a patient back to consciousness. "Hey there, mister!" she yelled at the boy's face. "Do you hear me? What's your name?" She waited for the patient to react then straightened up, head shaking. "This boy, he's not just unconscious. He's in a coma. Can't feel a thing."

"He ain't gonna die on us, is he?" the deputy said as if the possibility was out of line.

Nurse Parker stood staring at the boy, her fists on her hips. In the past, she'd handle all kinds of walk-ins who came in thinking the clinic was a hospital. She'd learned how to suture most wounds, control hemorrhages, set broken bones, stitch up wounds on children and victims of household accidents and minor car crashes on US 1. Not to mention mending cuts and broken heads from Saturday night brawls at the Tiki bars. But never a coma emergency. "I'm sorry, can't do a thing for him here. You've got to get him to a hospital."

"Then you better call Dr. Levin to come and get him," the deputy started to say.

"Me? Come on, Ray. Just put him in your truck and run him to Venetian Shores."

The deputy winced. "What, with all the hoopla over at Munson and Ramrod Keys with the Hollywood movie people? Hell, I've been off duty for over two hours already. I shouldn't even be here now."

"Look, all I can give you is my opinion," she said. "And I'm telling you this boy could stop breathing at any time. He'll die on that table if he's not taken to a proper hospital. Now."

The deputy put on his cap. "I'm calling Sheriff Spotswood. Where do you keep the phone?"

"There," Nurse Parker said pointing at the desk. "Where it's always been."

The deputy pushed the cat off the chair, sat down, picked up the receiver and dialed zero with his thick index finger. Then he glanced up at the ceiling waiting for an answer.

"Betty, it's me, Ray," he said into the telephone. "I'm in Tavernier at Dr. Cohn's . . . OK. You? Good. Listen, can you put me through to the sheriff right away?" He paused, listening. "I know he's with those movie folks but I got an emergency situation here . . . Yes, the life and death kind . . . Has anything come in from headquarters, the Coast Guard, anything? Any boating accident report in our area? No? Can you check?" He waited, rubbing his cropped head. "Nothing? All right . . . Me? Drive him to Florida City? Can't do it today . . . OK, thanks, see what you can do."

The telephone rang soon after. Sheriff Spotswood calling. The deputy stood up to take the call.

Nurse Parker and Luther huddled around the desk, listening.

"Deputy Ray Tandy here . . . Yes sir, at Dr. Cohn's . . . Betty's right, a life and death situation. Looks like a near-drowning . . . Well, Nurse Parker says the subject's in a state of coma . . . Yes, I brought him myself. No, no idea who he is . . . Fishermen working the outer Keys found him at Dove . . . Oh, I got their IDs all right. The boy? Nothing on him, not even a tattoo." The deputy looked at what he'd written on his notepad. "Male Caucasian between eighteen and twenty-five. Maybe five-eleven, 160-170 pounds. No, no evidence of that. A few cuts and scratches from being out in the mangroves, I reckon. Yeah, it looks like he was there a while. Maybe since last night . . . No, no reports of boating accidents. Betty checked. He doesn't look like a refugee to me, sir, but . . . You're right, we can't exclude foul play . . . That's what Nurse Parker said, he's more dead than alive. But he is breathing—"

"Give me that." Nurse Parker took the telephone from the deputy's hand. "Hi, sheriff. Yes, it's me. Sir, it's like this: you either have someone rush him to a hospital now or in a couple of hours you'd be calling the coroner to take him away . . ."

Sheriff Spotswood, who was in the middle of an equally serious negotiation with a team of Hollywood producers scouting for locations in the Keys for a movie about President Kennedy, and about to settle on a rental price for his island to be used as the film's set, said he would take care of it.

As it happened, the sheriff instructed Betty, the telephone exchange operator, to find someone, anyone in her Rolodex to take the boy to a hospital, anywhere. After a series of calls, arrangements were made with the local Volunteer Corps to transfer the patient to Miami in the only vehicle available, a funeral hearse.

Before the volunteers arrived, Nurse Parker went into the examination room to make sure the boy was still alive. She gazed at his polished marble-like figure floating in the hot light over the metal table. His faint respiration was the only visible sign of life. From the sink, she brought a pale with lukewarm water to the table. She sponged his body carefully around his lesions and toweled him dry. Next, she fitted the BP cuff around his arm, slipped the stethoscope under it, and pumped the air valve. Then she let it go while listening to the whooshing as his blood flow resumed. Astonished, she watched how the meter spiked up higher and higher, stopping at 58/20. After his should-be-dead low reading earlier, she couldn't believe it. To make sure she'd done the procedure correctly, she tried it again. She retraced her motions one by one. And again both systolic and diastolic readings rose nearer to the standard range. It made her own heart race, thinking her touch had somehow made it happen. From the cabinet drawer, she pulled out a secondhand hospital gown and called Luther. Together they fitted the gown over the patient's nude body.

Luther kept smiling at his boss, aware of how much her satisfaction hinged on the wellbeing of those in her care. "He's sure nice and clean now."

"Just want him to look decent," she said. "Don't want people to talk."

"Yes, mam."

When the volunteers arrived, Nurse Parker watched them carry the boy out of the clinic from on top of the steps. Luther stood behind her, his arms crossed until the black hearse pulled away in a puff of gravel dust. Back inside the clinic, she put away her nurse's cap and lab coat in her locker and untied her hair. It fell straight over her shoulders. Something about this boy was staying with her, something she couldn't put into words but felt as real as her own beating heart.

"It sure is a pity, a good-looking boy like that," she heard Luther say as she locked the front door. "Who knows, maybe them Miami doctors will make him well."

"Maybe."

The gleaming black hearse pulled into the bright lights of the Jackson Memorial Hospital in Miami. Two man-nurses rushed out with a gurney and wheeled him inside. A mixture of pity and mystery rolled along with the unnamed patient into the white-tiled Emergency ward.

An hour later after the ICU team had him stabilized, he was left in the care of Nurse Angelo. A trio of staff nurses coming back from their breaks gathered around Nurse Angelo and watched her deterge the anonymous patient. The nurses, all females, made a few whispered comments on the extraordinary glow of his skin and well-proportioned body. "It's like he's made of polished plaster of Paris . . . Has anyone checked his back for wings, 'cause this boy looks just like an angel . . . A scratched up one, but mmm, an angel indeed, the poor thing . . ." another one compared him to a defaced Renaissance sculpture except for a prominent aspect of it that made the others giggle.

When the attending physician arrived to examine the patient, the nurses dispersed back to their stations.

After a quick evaluation, Dr. Michaels—a wiry short man in his mid-thirties who could've passed for a man even younger had he not conducted himself as smug as any of the veteran physicians in the hospital—sat at a desk in the vestibule and filled out his report on the unidentified teenager.

Being that the placeholder name of John Doe was presently taken by another unidentified patient, he asked the nurses for a name to call the new patient.

They answered almost in unison. "David."

"OK," he said, amused. "But David what?"

"Fine?" one nurse answered without thinking. "Yes . . . yes . . . Fine is fitting," the choir agreed.

So David Fine it was.

During the next twenty-four hours, a parade of officials came to see the unidentified white male that had washed ashore in the Keys. The first ones to show were two Miami Police detectives, who took his fingerprints and upset the staff with their smoking and the ink stains they left on the bedsheets and towels. A local councilman accompanied by a Dade County lawyer came before lunch, followed by two FBI agents who stayed only long enough to take his photograph. Several TV and newspaper reporters asked for and were denied access to his ICU room. Everyone wanted to know to whom the angelic young man belonged.

The following morning, every plausible theory of David Fine's origin and the probable causes of how he ended up in a deserted key were debated on talk radio programs and newspaper editorials. Every imaginable scenario was discussed—an accident in the high seas, a suicide gone awry, a sailor fallen overboard from some passing vessel, a botched kidnapped victim left to die, a marooned refugee escaping from communist Cuba; as well as the least logical ones, such as a drowning swimmer rescued by dolphins, or the mysterious doings of mermaids, or the Bermuda Triangle . . . .

The following evening, Nurse Parker came home from work and gazed across her backyard at the orange and blue sunset over her little piece of oceanfront. Too late for the swim she'd hoped for, she sat down on a metallic chair by the screen door and switched on her transistor. In the Keys, time moved slower than painkillers, she was given to say. Days overlapped on each other until she couldn't tell them apart. Today could've been yesterday or the day before, if not for the castaway boy.

She sipped her virgin iced tea-lemonade and smoked a Kent while listening to the news. She couldn't get the image of the boy out of her head. Even the crackling voice on the radio was going on about him. No one seemed to know who he was or where he came from. The issue of his identity hadn't even crossed her mind until then. It seemed entirely reasonable to her, given what happened between them. The steamy rainbow that formed before her eyes, which apparently only she saw, and the way his blood pressure rose as if by magic after she bathed him. The out of the blue feeling that washed over her, the sense of having experienced a revelation, which after a whole day still tremored within her. No, she didn't need to know who he is. Do marvels need a background check? The thought made her smile.

Nurse Parker listened to the radio until the mosquitoes chased her back indoors. In the kitchen she heated up the conch chowder Fannie, her neighbor down the road, had brought her. She stirred it slowly on the fire, thinking she should call the Jackson Memorial Hospital and find out how the boy was doing. Then decided against it, wary of how it might reflect on her at the clinic. She wasn't sure of what Dr. Cohn and Dorothy might think if they found out she was following up on a non-paying patient. She could imagine the many ways it could set their suspicious minds working.

She opened a can for Mister and emptied it in his bowl. She set her bowl of chowder with a side dish of diced avocado from her tree on the two-chair table and had her meal. Her rabbit-ears TV was on the only channel it picked up. The local newscaster was reporting on the 'unidentified youth found in Dove Key.' She got up and turned up the volume. Sheriff Spotswood appeared briefly on camera, taking the credit for the rescue. She laughed in silence, imagining of how Ray the deputy—who'd thought himself the hero of the day—must be feeling about it. The boy was famous. She put the dishes in the sink, wondering if she would ever see him again.

Out on the front porch, Nurse Parker eased on the rocking chair under the ceiling fan. Her Johnny Mathis record album was playing. A patch of stars flickered through the nebula of the window screen. Thinking of the boy made her feel less alone. It stirred up feelings in her she thought gone for a long time, together with others she never felt before. Chances are, she sang to herself, she'd call the hospital tomorrow and inquire about him. Why shouldn't she?

The identity of the young comatose stranger became the topic of the day for the staff at the Jackson Hospital. For Dr. Michaels and Nurse Angelo, the issue of his identity was of secondary concern. The doctor was awestruck by the patient's extraordinary response to his alleged near-drowning. After twenty-four hours, the patient exhibited none of the clinical signs associated with fluid aspiration or hypothermia or hypoxia. And while his condition could not be diagnosed in any other way but as a state of coma, he showed no evidence of decorticate rigidity—the mummy baby posture—or extensor posturing, the symptoms associated with most comatose patients. He could even do without the ventilator to help him breathe. Dr. Michaels began to think that he might have stumbled on a patient in possession of a unique constitution, much more resilient than that of the average patient, an organism worthy of deeper study.

It fired up his interest in a way that reminded him of why he'd chosen medicine as his life's work. "I'm telling you," he said to Nurse Angelo as he checked the EEG's metal discs and the rest of the equipment attached to the patient. "The numbers don't lie. I've never seen anything like it."

Nurse Angelo, a long-boned woman, taller than the doctor, answered with a silent grin.

"I can't think of anything else we can do with him." The doctor shook his head, smiling. "All this boy needs to stay alive is a conservative dose of glucose to control his hypotension, some antibiotics intravenously twice a day, a comfortable bed, and he's as good as asleep. What worries me," he said with his smile fading. "Time is not on his side. No matter how strong his heart is. If he doesn't wake up in three days or so, he's bound to remain in a coma indefinitely—a vegetable." The doctor waved his clipboard at his nurse and walked toward the door. "See you in the morning."

"Have a good night, doctor," Nurse Angelo said.

By seven a.m., Nurse Parker was out in the porch having breakfast, dressed to go to work. Looking out of the aluminum mesh windows, she could see her rusting 1956 Chevrolet convertible parked on the weed and gravel in front of the door. Behind it was dusty Ogygia Street. She grabbed her purse and the bag with her nursing clogs and walked to the clinic. Mister followed her like a dog to the clinic except on rainy days, and sometimes only as far as US 1 whenever he sensed Dorothy would be there.

Like Mister, she didn't walk when it rained. She drove instead. But only because she could lose her shoes in the sandy mud roadside. There were no sidewalks or curbs in her part of Tavernier. Urban development wasn't something the Conchs believe in all that much. Anything that would derail their laid-back life was a thumbs-down for them, delayed forever. She was OK with it, though. After six years, she'd been able to find something akin to contentment in her rented zinc-roof bungalow by the Gulf. It more than made up for the wild surges of weather, the frequent power blackouts, and the quirky locals who had unnerved her so when she first arrived. The Florida Keys had been as far as she could get from Portland, Maine, without moving away from the sea and still be able to make a living. She had her neighbors to thank for it. The Conchs may not have believed in many things but they believed in what they saw. In their end-of-the-line world, this meant if you told them you could do something and did it to their satisfaction, then, in their eyes, you were the real thing—even a professional nurse with or without a license. No more questions asked.

On the turnoff to U.S. 1, Fannie's husband, Marvin, honked his car horn when he drove past her. Out of the corner of her eye, she saw him wink at her from behind the wheel—the bug head.

As the sole full-time nurse at Dr. Cohn's clinic, Nurse Parker had become a local of note because of her professional qualities and her reputation of being punctual, a rare characteristic among the natives. Slim and physically shaped by her athletic past, keeping the women-starved Conchs in line was another story. She'd been able to handle it so far, she thought, at least outwardly so. Raised in a house outnumbered by males of every age had prepared her well for the everyday of it. The severity of her presence also had something to do with it. So much so that after her first year or so the local housewives had gone from resenting her for her figure, fearing for their men, to accepting her as one of them, even pitying her solitude.

When she arrived, Dorothy, Dr. Cohn's wife was already there, sitting at his desk 'minding the store.' The doctor came in later after the patients began arriving.

After a polite good morning exchange, Nurse Parker busied herself setting up the medical instruments for the doctor. In the consultation room, she glanced at the empty white table and the image of the boy, the man—she hadn't decided—appeared before her eyes. It froze her in place, but the vision faded before she could catch her breath. She'd never been the type who believed in spirits and superstition, but reason had little to do with it this time. What did it mean? Was he dead? Had he died? Was his ghost reaching out to her, haunting her? She felt the tremoring inside her again, a funny agitation heating up.

For the rest of the day, whenever Dr. Cohn stepped away from his desk, she'd look at the telephone, tempted to sneak a call to the Jackson Hospital. She wanted so much to ask how the boy was doing. But each time she held herself back. For the sake of her job, she told herself.

That evening, at home, she was again paralyzed by her strange hesitancy whenever she glanced at her telephone. She listened to the newscast on the radio and the five o'clock news on TV. But the castaway boy wasn't news anymore—Marilyn

Monroe singing Happy Birthday to President Kennedy was all that mattered.

Later in bed, cocooned inside the gauzy shadows of the mosquito netting, the vision of the castaway boy lodged in her head. The sharper his presence became, the harder her heart pounded. Her thoughts turned and turned again like the humid breaths from the ocean thrusting through the blinds, slurping the air out of the room.

Until tonight, it had been her ex-husband who her mind wandered to when her need arose, the one she thought of—seven years apart had not been long enough to change that. She'd known others, sure. But when it came down to it, he was the only one who could ward off the memory of that other one, the alcohol-reeking shadow that materialized in her corner bed in the middle of the night while her brothers pretended to sleep. The foul-smelling fiend who'd broken her, made her life miserable and forced her to exile from herself. Tonight, it was different. It was the image of the beatific man-boy. The quiet storm with which he'd taken over her thoughts, the feel of his flesh pulsing to life in her hands, the liquid rainbow that joined them together.

For two days, Dr. Michaels and Nurse Angelo remained by the patient's bedside. Together, they monitored and recorded his vital signs every hour. With the help of the hospital specialists, they ruled out one by one the possible causes of his state of coma. They found no evidence the patient had suffered a seizure or a stroke, detected no sign of brain swelling or bleeding, no infection or an accidental accumulation of toxins. Even drowning, the most probable cause of the oxygen deprivation event to blame for his coma seemed dismissible. The patient's natural capacity to self-sustain challenged all the existing data on Dr. Michael's medical books.

On his day off, the doctor drove to the hospital determined to put into effect a new-fangled treatment on precipitating conscious awareness on comatose subjects. It entailed having those closest to the patient—in this case, themselves, for lack of known kin—to read him from books and play music the patient might be familiar with as a way to revive recognizable sensations.

"But what if he speaks another language?" Nurse Angelo felt compelled to point out. "What then?"

"I know that's one obstacle," Dr. Michaels told her, thinking he still could make it work. "The important thing is to make a human connection with the patient. Expose him to the sound of a caring voice, the feel of affection. It's worth a try. What do we have to lose?"

It took Dr. Michaels but a few tries at reading and talking to the patient to realize the futility of trying to reach an unconscious, complete stranger. Stooped shouldered, the doctor packed up the portable record player and the records albums he never got to play and placed the books back in his attaché. Before leaving he said to Nurse Angela, "The problem is the longer a state of coma extends, the greater the likelihood of residual symptoms. Particularly physical disabilities, brain damage."

"I wouldn't count this boy out just yet, doctor," Nurse Angelo told him with her nun-like grin. "As you know, plenty of comatose patients make good recoveries. It wouldn't surprise me one bit if our a.k.a. David Fine here turns out to be one of those. His color's coming back. He breathes like an angel. It's like the rules don't apply to him."

Dr. Michaels let out a long sigh. "From your lips to God's ears."

By noon on Saturday, Nurse Parker had finished seeing her regulars at the clinic—neither Dr. Cohn nor his wife came on weekends if they could help it. She took the tin of Spanish dulce de leche Mrs. Gomez—who came to her for daily insulin shots—had brought her. She sent Luther home, hung the sign with the emergency telephone numbers on the clinic's door, and locked up for the day.

As was her habit whenever she came home early, Nurse Parker put on her bathing suit and swam out to the coral reef across the water from her backyard, her piece of the lazy Gulf of Mexico. From shore, the islet looked like a caricature of a shipwreck's island, a knob over the water with a single midget palm tree in the middle of some undergrowth. Nurse Parker, without missing her stride, swung her arm over the water, touched a mound of coral jutting over the surface, and free-styled back toward shore to complete the mile.

A pink and blue sunset glowed behind her when she strode back to her bungalow, a white towel wrapped like a creampuff over her head. Her skin tingled with positive energy. She kicked off her slippers by the back door. Barefoot, she walked on the linoleum floor of the kitchen to the carpeting of her bedroom and on to the tile of the bathroom.

In the shower, she caught herself humming some tune that sounded familiar to her but she didn't recognize. She wondered if she'd made it up. After another go at it, she realized she'd been merging the 'Jamaica Farewell' song and the Limbo song melodies together. Odin, her ex-husband, used to call her his Calypso girl because she was crazy about Harry Belafonte and limbo dancing in those days. She cut the water and stepped out of the steamy stall.

She towel-dried her hair in front of the full-body mirror on the door.

The flaws that had affected her so as a young girl seemed to benefit her at forty-one, she thought. Her slight curves had softened rounder, filled out into an agreeable silhouette. The firmness of her breasts held reasonably well too, so did her thigh gap—two aspects of her figure she prided in. Her blonde hair had grown darker despite the grays but remained as plentiful as it was in her teenage years. She ignored the triangular patch of sunburned skin on her chest under her neck to avoid upsetting her mood—no matter how much cream she put on it, it never went away. Her face, well . . . she'd gone years blocking out her nose as part of her face when in front of a mirror. The same as with the two pinkish lines of her lips that made her look permanently pissed. If she had something to look at it was her body. Maybe her eyes too, 'emerald blue like the beaches in heaven,' as Odin had put it in a Valentine's Day card when they started going out . . . the castaway boy's eyes were also blue, she remembered.

It would've been so much easier if she were able to get the boy out of her thoughts, stop her mind from obsessing about him. But thinking of him only compelled her to think more about him.

She slipped into a white T-shirt and a pair of cutoff jeans. In a sudden rush of determination, she marched toward her telephone in the living room. She went as far as dialing the first three numbers of the Jackson Hospital before she dropped the receiver back on the cradle. Furious with herself, she stomped to the kitchen and opened a can of tuna for Mister. She scooped it out in his bowl, then slapped a ham and cheese sandwich together for herself and ate it with angry bites, leaning against the counter.

Back in Portland, she wouldn't have thought it twice driving to the Seven Eleven for a six-pack and putting up with the taste of beer to numb her brain. But that too she'd given up, drinking—the 'Keys Disease,' Dr. Cohn called it—because of her job.

She took the first record album on the pile, laid it on the turntable and flipped the play lever. Out in the porch, she dropped on the rocking chair for her nightly ritual of chamomile tea and Kent cigarettes. A three-month-old American Journal of Nursing magazine sat on the side table. She didn't feel like reading, not in her state of mind. Not even Mrs. Gomez's extremely sugary dulce de leche—actually hard-boiled condensed milk—could sweeten her mood now. She hated her indecision; how it made her feel. It was more than job security that was holding her back from making the call. More than what people might say if they were to find out. Something on the far side of herself she was too scared to face was stopping her. A hidden woe that she would probably have condemned as too self-indulgent had it not been happening to her.

Nurse Parker looked away at the night shadows beyond the smoky window screen. Solitude was her real addiction, her personal disease. It was both what she needed and what killed her. The Platters record was playing. The song that always touched her in spite of the sappy lyrics was coming on. The music embraced her; the singer's voice breathed in her ear, spun her and seized her tighter until a teardrop rolled down her cheek. She couldn't help it. Had there been anyone around she would've blamed it on the cigarette smoke stinging her eye—or better yet, on every woman's right to cry whether she's happy or sad or both, or for nothing at all. She saw her own reflection magnified in the liquid welling in her eyes, the one who supposed to be her but was not . . .

"Gotta gift for yah." She heard Odin's voice.

"What?"

"You heard me. Here, open it."

"Whatever for?"

"Can't see it, if you don't open it. Got it at Bean's."

"I mean, why did you get me a present?"

"As an expression my love, darling."

She unwrapped the package. In it was the tiniest two-piece swimsuit she'd ever seen. "A leopard-print bikini?"

"So you have something new to wear Saturday night." He was referring to a party the guys from his office had planned.

It took her but one second to realize why he had bought it. Insane with fury, she ripped up the box it came in and almost tore the "gift" itself to shreds had he not yanked it from her hands in time. He'd gotten it only to show her off—her body that is—to his friends from work. The same ones she'd once heard whispering behind her, "she'd be perfect with a paper bag over her head."

"Not a fucking chance," she remembered shouting at him.

She wore it to the party anyway, in a sort of reverse spite. It still made her blood boil when she thought about it. But back then . . . back then it hurt like a harpoon through her heart . . . It happened at Willard Beach, during a California-style beach party like in the movies in the limbo-crazed summer . . . the music blasting through outdoor horn speakers . . . people she knew and people she didn't know dancing in a boozed-up haze on the sand around the bonfire . . . Somebody announced a limbo contest . . . When her turn came up everybody formed a circle around her . . . They clapped, hollered and cheered watching her move under the limbo stick, lower than any of them ever could . . . Do it again they yelled and she did it again and again, lower and lower . . . her knees bent, her sweaty buttocks scraping the sand, midriff glistening in the light of the blazing fire, her breasts half bulging out of the bikini top with her every thrust . . . the lower they set the bar, the louder they hollered . . . "How low can you go" . . . Everybody loved her and she loved them right back, any and all. Until Odin found her coming out of a boathouse with two of his friends . . . "You wanted to know how low I can go? Well, now you know."

It marked the end of what she once believed would last forever.

It still sickened her to remember despite the years, the balled up cruelty that spewed out of her that night, the hemorrhage of self-loathing. Neither Odin nor she deserved it, of course. It was all directed to a person who wasn't even living by then, the shadow demon of her nightmares.

The next day at the clinic before the doctor arrived, Nurse Parker walked straight to Dr. Cohn's desk. She picked up the telephone and dialed the number of the Jackson Memorial in Miami. Luther watched her from the doorway, his sweaty head bowed as if not listening. She got Dr. Michaels on the line without any trouble. She introduced herself. "Yes, Nurse Parker from Dr. Cohn's clinic."

When she heard the doctor say the patient was alive, Nurse Parker had to cover her lips with her free hand. "I see," she managed to say.

"He remains in a state of coma, but he's stable. Showing some progress," Dr. Michaels said.

"So glad to hear it, doctor. Has any family member come to see him yet, anyone?"

"Well, Miss Parker, we were hoping you could tell us something about that. As far as we know, his identity remains a mystery."

"I'm sorry, doctor. The men who rescued him found nothing in the way of identification with him."

"That's what the police told us. His fingerprints and photograph haven't yielded anything, so far. The FBI hasn't been able to find any record of him. Not until some next of kin of his turns up, his identity will remain unknown, I'm afraid."

"Doctor, what do you think will happen if no one comes to claim him?"

"It depends. If he remains in a coma, he'll be transferred to another facility. If he's lucky and wakes up within a reasonable time, he himself will tell us who he is."

"Of course."

"Anyway," the doctor went on. "Let's hope he gets well soon. We can only imagine how his family must be feeling. His present condition aside, he does seem well taken care of."

Although Nurse Parker's conversation with Dr. Michaels ended cordially and with an opened invitation to visit the patient at any time, it distressed her in ways she couldn't have fathomed. Why had no one claimed him? She hadn't counted on that. What an awful thought, she realized. That someone could claim him. That he belonged somewhere, to someone. Until then, she hadn't imagined him having a past. He had appeared in her life fully formed, brand new, just as she thought of him: a gift from the sea. But now the idea of someone showing up to claim him and take him away . . . God, what if that were to happen?

After three days in the ICU and in spite of the mounting pressure from the hospital's administration, Dr. Michaels refused to give up on his notorious patient. He called for a morning meeting with the specialists. "Since day zero," he told them, "David Fine has shown us he's by no means a textbook case. And, yes, we've done everything we could do for him. And, as the administration's made very clear, every day he remains in the ICU is an expense the hospital might not recoup. But there's so much more we can learn about his condition. We have to keep him here a bit longer. I say, let's take advantage of the opportunity this patient is offering us. Gentlemen, all we have to do is keep him as healthy as we can until he himself shows us how to proceed. It's not over yet, and we know it . . . A few more days in the ICU might mean the world to him and science."

The specialists glanced at each other, made some remarks concerning their busy schedules, but compelled by Dr. Michael's zeal they finally concurred.

Twenty-four hours later, David Fine remained immovable in his stable condition like a breathing museum sculpture. The novelty of his extraordinary anatomy and mysterious origin began to wear off as the monotony of it set in. By the fourth day, the nurses who from the first day had been dropping by to check on him on their way home stopped coming. On Friday, the EEG monitor was disconnected. The specialists, claiming other priorities, did not return for follow-ups during the weekend. Dr. Michaels and Nurse Angelo stayed by the patient's side all the time they could, but their own enthusiasm started to run out as well. On Monday morning, the hospital administration announced that 'due to the likelihood the patient's comatose state would continue indefinitely,' he was to be transferred out of the ICU to a room on the second floor.

By then, even Nurse Parker's surprise visit failed to renew any interest in the case. Chased by a tropical downpour, she'd entered the hospital doors running, clutching a dozen red roses inside wet wrapping paper. She had expected to be received with some curiosity—after all, who'd want to visit an unidentified patient? But when she stood at the front desk the opposite happened. The young woman behind the counter gave her a routine smile and asked her, "Do you know which room Mr. Fine is in?"

"Sorry, I don't"

"Umm, let me see." The young woman shuffled the papers on her desk until she found the right one. "Oh," she said, looking up at Nurse Parker. "I think you better have a seat."

"Is there a problem?"

"No, well, to see this patient you must be accompanied by a staff member. Hospital's rules." She pointed at the waiting area. "Please."

Nurse Parker walked to the empty bench near the wall. A few faces aimed her way when she sat down. The inside of her tall-heeled shoes felt like soaked squeegees. It had been one flash downpour after another the entire drive from Tavernier until she reached Homestead, where she stopped at a flower shop. Then, after crossing the last drawbridge into northwest Miami, it started pouring even harder. She couldn't find a parking space near the Jackson Hospital area and had to leave the car in an opened lot a few streets' distance. Outside in the downpour, she couldn't find the umbrella she kept in the trunk. She'd had no choice but to sprint with her purse over her head, shortcutting over waterlogged lawns and puddles, all the way to the hospital's entrance.

The standing fan in the visitors' waiting area kept swiveling in her direction, blowing bursts of cold air. She moved to another bench, afraid she'd catch a cold. Her circle skirt clung to her legs like a second skin. She wrung the hemline to stop it from dripping. Out of her purse, she pulled the powder case and looked in the small round mirror. The curls that had required the torture of sleeping with eight hair rollers now hung like wet fringes around her face. She let out a weepy sigh wondering what else could go wrong.

An imposing, lanky nurse in a starch-stiff white uniform approached her. "Nurse Parker?"

"Yes."

"Hi, I'm Head Nurse Angelo. So nice to meet you."

"Likewise," Nurse Parker said. "Mam, is everything all right?"

Nurse Angelo gave her a mother superior smile. "Absolutely."

"All this security," she said.

"David's under special supervision, you understand. Come, I'll walk you to his room."

"But he is OK?"

"He's doing as well as expected."

They walked together deeper into the hospital smell of the Jackson and up to the second floor, making their acquaintances as they went, neither wanting it to become any more personal than it had to be. At the end of a quiet corridor, Nurse Angelo signaled with one hand. "Here we are. You go right ahead. I'll see if I can find a vase for the roses."

Nurse Parker handed her the flowers, the wet wrapping disintegrating in her hand. "Thank you."

Nurse Parker stepped into the hush of the room, her eyes adjusting to the dimness. Slowly, she approached the figure inside the whiteness on the bed.

When she at last found herself by his side, she needed to catch her breath. She focused with all her senses on the little of him there was to see under the bed dressing. She gazed at his serene facial features, so familiar to her thoughts now. In her mind, she again saw every part of him the sheets hid from her eyes, the flawless topography of his skin, the secret life that pulsed in his slumbering body. She called him with her thoughts, hoping for a gesture, a sign, an indicator of what she should do with all she was feeling inside her. When she could no longer restrain herself, she caressed his face and felt his cold skin warming to her touch. A smile formed at the ends of her lips as she gazed at the butterfly-wing delicateness of his breathing, the contour of his chest under the sheet, barely moving with his minimal respiration. She listened to his silence until she lost track of time.

The door opened behind her. Nurse Angelo entered and set the vase with the red roses by his bed. "They're very pretty," she said.

Nurse Parker had to fake not wiping her tears. "Yes, thanks."

"I'll wait here," Nurse Angelo said from the doorway.

Nurse Parker nodded and smiled, but the spell was broken, the moment ruined. It no longer was just the two of them. It amazed her how quickly her feelings changed when he and she weren't alone together.

Feeling the head nurse's presence behind her, she thought she'd been there long enough but couldn't move away from him. She stood as in prayer, breathing the air between them, matching his stillness, letting her soul rest side by side with his.

With a polite cough, Nurse Angelo announced viewing time was over.

Nurse Parker kissed the tip of her fingers and with a quick movement of her hand touched his lips softly.

Nurse Parker drove back to the Keys in a state of grace. As she traversed the Seven Mile Bridge, the windshield wipers thumped in double time and the rain beat on the car roof loud but it was all good, all fine. She needed no more proof of anything to know what she had to do. Nothing had ever made her feel the way she felt in his nearness—the happy chaos in her soul, the pleasure of trusting without having to understand. It intensified her faith in him. How she had come to this conclusion, she no longer needed to know. To think of him in any other way would only crush her.

By the time she reached Ogygia Street, the road was almost dry.

At home, she looked under the sink and found the bottle of white wine a patient had given her as a Christmas gift. She poured herself a glass and took a walk out to the caprock shore, feeling much like the Calypso Queen of old. The sunset shone in neon streaks between the ashen sky and the leaden Gulf. She raised her glass and drank to the clouds and the rain. In her early days in the Keys, she missed the change of seasons. Maine's winter snow, the fall foliage, the thrill of spring, the summertime blithe. Now, she thought there was nothing like those coral rocks strewn over the ocean. Where else could she watch the sunrise over the Atlantic in the morning, take a walk to the opposite shore at day's end, and see the sunset over the Gulf?

In the kitchen, she took out of the refrigerator the two two-pounder trout she'd picked up at the pier on the way home. She cleaned and cooked them outside on the cinderblock grill, with a shot of wine, butter, garlic, and lemon. Mister stood in full alert pacing between her legs throughout the process. When the fish was done, they shared it together. She sat at the table and Mister munched it out of his bowl with his back to her. She smiled at his upturned tail. It reminded her of herself. Being a loner is not the same as being selfish.

She refilled her wine glass and went out on the front porch. It didn't occur to her to play a record. She leaned back on the rocker and listened to the sounds of the night. She made herself laugh imagining what she would do with an eighteen-year-old in the house. How would she explain that? A gift from the sea wasn't going to work once the Conchs found out. Word of it would spread like the plague. She could apply for foster parenthood, she told herself as a joke. Then she thought about it in earnest. It might be possible if he's not yet eighteen. But what if he is older? A legal adult. With a gymnast's body like his? He might well be. Eighteen . . . he'd have to register with the Selective Service. That didn't make her feel so good—although he'd be a knockout in uniform. She again laughed thinking she could adopt him. She didn't think there was an age limit to adoption. Worse comes to worst, they could move away together. Elope. They could relocate to Key West, which might not be far away enough but at least she'd be able to find a job there. In the Conch capital, it would be easier to blend in, and her nursing credentials would be up to standard. She emptied the bottle of wine in her glass.

"To you, David Fine," she said, raising her glass. "However old you are."

She rather liked the name they'd given him in the hospital. If she adopted him legally, he'd most likely become David Parker. She liked the sound of this one too. It had a classic ring to it. Sharing the same last name, people might mistake him for her brother, or her son. Well, not necessarily. Some might take him for her husband. This too was possible. Twenty years' age difference isn't so much, nowadays. Like hell is not. But hey, she told herself, if she was going to let her imagination fly, then might as well let it skyrocket all the way. The real difference would be up to him, really. She could be whatever he wanted her to be, his friend, his partner, his lover. She could be all of them together if he wanted to. One thing was without a doubt—even if he didn't know it yet—something greater than both of them had brought them together and there was no going back, not anymore. She was his as he was hers.

Nurse Parker went to bed and fell out the instant her head hit the pillow.

Sometime after midnight of the seventh day, while Dr. Michaels sat reading at David Fine's bedside, he happened to glance up from his book and notice the patient's REM had increased tremendously. It was as if the boy was seeing a panorama full of motion under his closed eyelids.

"Sofia," he called Nurse Angelo. "Have you seen him do that before? His eyeballs moving like this?"

"I haven't, no."

Dr. Michaels and Nurse Angelo looked closer at their patient and then at each other. "Could it be?" she asked.

The doctor didn't answer right away, but his nurse could tell he'd also taken it as a positive sign. He reflected for a few moments, staring at his patient with an expression of weighty expectation. "I think we should prepare ourselves for an over-night vigil," he finally said.

The next tease came at daybreak when the first sunrays from the window reached David's bed. They noticed his thumb twitching slightly, his eyelids squinting, almost opening with the movement of his eyeballs.

At first, Dr. Michaels was reluctant to do anything other than observe without interfering, his strategy from the start. He wanted the patient to return to consciousness through a natural process, and track its development for his records. But as the morning unfolded, word of the patience's upturn got around the ward and he began to contemplate hastening the process.

Nurses coming off duty drifted into the room to join the watch. Dr. Michaels allowed them as long as they kept silent and followed his orders. It was his show and they agreed right away.

At midday, a silent excitement took hold of the room when they saw his Adam's apple move and his arms and feet twitch under the sheets, followed by a series of involuntary leg spasms and muscle contractions.

"Discharges of neuromuscular tension," Dr. Michaels said to the nurses gathered around him.

"What does it mean, doctor?"

"It may be the time has come," he said, holding back from mentioning the other possibility: that the patient may be dying.

Dr. Michaels called Nurse Angelo aside and told her to bring a technician to fit the patient with an oxygen mask. "He doesn't need it right now, but it won't hurt either."

The second-floor nurses were joined by several others from the ICU on their lunch break. Dr. Michaels took a break alone in his private office. With the patient all to themselves, the nurses got busy grooming him in anticipation of his awakening, to make him presentable to himself. They clipped his nails, deterged his skin with scented alcohol, changed his dressing, combed his hair—as shaving was unnecessary, the blondish fuzz over his upper lip was almost invisible. Lastly, they slipped him into a fresh hospital gown.

When Dr. Michaels returned, he found an even larger group of nurses standing around in the room. Nurse Angelo was sitting by the side of the bed holding the patient's hand. "What's going on?" he asked.

The nurses answered at the same time. "He grimaced . . . he cried . . . he rolled his eyes . . . he's been gurgling and grunting like a baby."

"He seems to be having a little trouble breathing," Nurse Angelo said.

"That's because his airways are probably filled with secretion. Let's clear them up."

"I'll take care of it." Nurse Angelo stood up. "Bring me an oral suction tip," she said to one of the nurses.

"He's perspiring quite a bit too," another one said.

A frown formed in the doctor's face. He hadn't been expecting that but kept it to himself. He dried the patient's forehead with cotton. "Has he opened his eyes or made any purposeful movement, tried to talk, anything of the sort?"

Nurse Angelo shook her head.

An hour later, the patient's body began to shudder inside the cocoon of bedsheets. The nurses called Dr. Michaels who was outside on the phone. He flew in the room.

Nurse Angelo said, "He made a guttural-like noise, doctor. It sounded like he was trying to say something."

"Could it just have been moaning?" Doctor Michaels asked.

"Yes, but there was something to it," his nurse said. "I think he's transitioned to a more conscious state." The nurses along the wall nodded in concordance.

At that moment, the patient's body began to convulse, his hips thrusting up, limbs stiffening. It threw the nurses into a silent panic. Nurse Angelo, unable to hold herself any longer, rushed to the patient's side and shouted at his face. "Hey there young man, can you hear me? Come on look at me. Open your eyes. I know you can hear me. What's your name?" She swabbed his dry lips with a wet cotton ball. "Wake up. Look at me—"

"Come on, boy," one of the nurses joined in. "I know you can do it. Come on, tell us your name?"

Nurse Angelo turned to the doctor. "His breathing sounds even more labored."

"Someone, raise the bed," Dr. Michaels said, moving into action. He pulled the oxygen tank closer and fitted the mask on the patient himself.

A nurse cranked up the head of the bed. The doctor snapped his fingers a few times in front of David's nose. "Hey there, buddy, can you hear me? You got a name, don't you? Come on wake up. Open your eyes . . ." His creation, his miracle patient, he wasn't going to let him die. "Wake up, son. I know you can hear me."

Every light in the room was on, the blinds rolled up for daylight. The entire group huddled tighter around the bed and joined the chant. "Wake up . . . You can do it." They rubbed his arms, his legs, and caressed his cheeks.

A big aaah resounded when his eyelids jerked in an attempt at opening. The nurses looked at each other openmouthed. He was almost there.

"Come on, sweetie. What's your name?" Their calls kept getting louder, more boisterous with every one of David's movements. "Come on. You can do it . . ."

The clamor reached the hospital's front desk downstairs. A security officer was dispatched to find out what was going on. He dashed to the elevator. When the doors slid open on the second floor, a sudden silence stopped him in the hallway.

The guard stepped around the corner toward where the shouting had been coming from. He halted midway upon seeing several nurses walking arm in arm out of David Fine's room, wiping their tears. Their quiet sobs were the only sound.

# TWO

*The viscous blackness was everything, a natural force, unmanageable. Within it, I was without form, without a body, part of the pitch-dark nothingness. Unrecognizable black shapes appeared and disappeared twirling like yet unformed ghosts over the blacker horizon.*

*The thin sound of a woman's cry, a maternal call, a supplication, swelled out of the great silence.*

*I could not understand it. I could not respond with any part of me. The cries multiplied, grew louder than my own respiration. It blended with a sensation of touch that confused me in a pleasant way. I became aware of my extremities, of my chest, of the air scraping in and out of my nostrils.*

*With my whole being, I sensed an outside.*

*A blinding glare flashed through my gashed eyelids and a blur of colors and figures formed around me. A half-circle of silhouettes, a carousel of them, stood bobbing in the luminous nearness. A misfire of the senses? I could not comprehend what their cries meant but I heard them. My eyelids flickered and I realized I could sustain my vision. Had I gone over the edge of conjecture? All my physical components seemed to be in on it. Rapid, shallow breaths entered and exited my lungs without me trying. My head throbbed as if just to prove its own existence; my limbs were there too but they didn't respond to thoughts of motion; a sickening taste invaded my mouth with the slightest shift of my tongue.*

*I understood then I was no longer where I'd been . . .*

The late afternoon sun slanted into the glass window shades of Dr. Cohn's clinic. His wife, Dorothy, gave Nurse Parker her Friday envelope. "You're off tomorrow, huh?" she said.

"Happens every three weeks," Nurse Parker answered as she counted the cash in the small manila envelope—four twenty-dollar bills, a five, a single and three quarters: $86.75.

"Have any plans?"

"Just driving north to visit friends." Nurse Parker slipped the envelope in her purse.

"To Miami? Again? My," Dorothy said with a lilt of insinuation.

Nurse Parker gave her an askance look. "Have a good one, Dorothy."

"You too, Francis."

At home, Nurse Parker stood in front of the bathroom mirror. It was her first attempt at coloring her hair. She argued with herself all through the messy process. In college, she'd been among the girls who shunned makeup, a take-me-as-I-am realist, too busy a natural spirit to need artificial enhancements. Now she was ready to use all there was at her disposal.

She parted her hair with a comb searching for grays and applied the dye.

Afterward, she sat in a sunny patch in the backyard to dry her hair, a hairbrush and a hand-mirror on her lap. Of all her cousins, she had the prettiest hair. It was the only praise her mother ever gave her, growing up. "Fran's got enough beautiful hair for the three of you," she'd tell them. It still warmed her heart to remember it. She'd grown up believing her golden tresses to be her introductory card whenever there was no other, always the blonde sunshine girl. She intended to be that girl again.

On Saturday, she packed for an overnight stay and got dressed. On her way out, she emptied a can of cat food in Mister's bowl and checked herself in the mirror by the door. Blonde again, she smiled. She looked close enough to her younger self.

She drove north to the last filling station on the Overseas Highway where the attendant wouldn't recognize her. She gassed up her Chevy for the drive to Miami. As she steered away, she grinned recalling the first time she drove up to see him. How she'd doubted herself, gone as far as seriously questioning her sanity. What in the world was she doing? What would she say when the nurse at the reception desk asked her how was she related to the patient? She almost turned back after the bridge over Lake Surprise. This time a different set of emotions were pushing her onward, the sense of it no longer mattered. This time she was complying with a directive of fate issued the moment the rainbow joined them together. As true as divine intervention could get.

After the initial commotion of David Fine's awakening, Dr. Michaels and Nurse Angelo asked the visiting nurses to leave the room. A grin of accomplishment lit their faces when they found themselves alone with their creation. They spoke in whispers to maintain a calm atmosphere in the room.

"Should I order an EEG monitor?" she asked.

"I don't think we should interfere unless we have to," Doctor Michaels said. "He's been doing great without us. I do expect him to be drifting in and out of consciousness for a time before becoming fully alert. Although, with him, who knows?"

Nurse Angelo nodded in silence.

The doctor clipped his stethoscope around his neck and pulled out his penlight. "All right, young man, let's see how you're doing this afternoon." He leaned fore and thumbed the patient's eyelid open, shone the light in one eye and then the other. Then he noticed both of the patient's eyes stayed open, looking back at him. "Holy crap," he let out, taking a quick step backward. "Are you seeing this?"

"He's wide awake," Nurse Angelo said. "Why doesn't he try to speak?"

"Too soon. But just look at him, Sofia. He's watching us."

Nurse Angelo tilted her head with a maternal grinned. "I wonder what he's seeing."

"Us, I hope," the doctor said. "Getting his bearing. Can't expect him to just wake up and say 'Where am I? It's not like that."

They laughed together in silence.

"This boy's been nothing but surprises," she said. "Why would it change now?"

"I think we shouldn't expect too much just yet, even from him. Post-coma recovery is slow. After what he's been through, it will be a gradual process. Then again, you're right. I wouldn't put it past him to get up and walk away."

Dr. Michaels and Nurse Angelo shared another silent laugh.

## THREE

My mind was a blank empty space, but in it I felt the full weight of my being. There was nothing where my memory had been, my eyesight, my hearing, the same as my thoughts, all my senses felt out of my control, yet they were there. Everything in sight seemed familiar and unfamiliar at the same time, inconclusive though solid. Pale blurs swam before me in the harsh light as if from behind a smudged glass. Their murmuring voices rose, faded and rose again. How I interpreted any of it, I knew not. It all came so unconditionally and with so little effort on my part, I couldn't question it. It just was.

As my vision adjusted, I focused on a glassy gadget, a syringe taped to my exposed arm. It was attached to a rubber tube connected to a baglike container hanging from a shiny tubular stand—it had the effect of linking me to my surroundings.

The name of objects came to me when I fixed my sight on them—the bedsheets, the ceiling lamp, the window, the clipboard hanging on the door . . . Perhaps this was how it was going to be from now on: I would first see the image, or feel it somehow before I remembered it. Identifying things in detail gave me a certain satisfaction. The clearer my vision became, the more I wanted to see.

An electric fan on the green and white wall exhaled currents of air on my face when it swiveled in my direction. Strips of bright light shone between the window shades. It made me look away. On the other side, I noticed two doors in the room. They were both ajar. Behind the narrower white one, there was a dark shadowed space; outside of the brown wider one, it glowed neon bright. Doors bore a certain significance I could not yet interpret.

People in white grinned at me as people do at newborns. I knew not how the image came to me, but it did. Reality was letting me in little by little.

I heard a chair scraping the floor and noticed a man's face leaning closer to me. He spoke in a language I could not understand. My brow tightened because of the glare coming through the window behind him, and his words. The woman in white stepped closer to me on the other side of the bed. She spoke softer, just above a whisper. I couldn't understand her either. The confusion it produced in me made my brow tightened harder. Had I not recognized and named the objects in the room? Had I not described them to myself? Something very strange was happening in my aching head. The air became harder to breathe. It upset me so the figures around me shuffled into action, speaking in loud, urgent voices. I passed out, fell-unconscious, fainted—whatever they called it.

I came around to the touch of someone's thumb stroking my forehead. The anxious faces from before were now calmly speaking amongst themselves, or so I thought. Then I realized they were speaking to me in their language. I couldn't understand anything. I felt confused, about to lose it again when all of a sudden the sound of a single utterance from the man in white brought me back. One word, two syllables did it: "OK."

He went on speaking but I didn't listen anymore. That single word, OK, filled my lungs with air again as if I'd been rescued from drowning. It clarified why I couldn't understand them. They were speaking in the language of the hundreds of subtitled movies I'd seen in my life . . . in the speak of my maestra de íngles . . . in the tongue of the singers on my phonograph records. I may not have known who I was or where I was, but I knew this much: they were speaking in English. And I had made it. Alive.

The feeling of well-being must have shown in my face. The figures in white looked at me, smiling at each other. I wanted to stay awake. I didn't want to be alone anymore. I wanted to talk. But my mouth was dry, parched. My tongue scraped over my cracked lips. Despite the turmoil in my head, I became conscious of what I needed. I could feel my thirst readying me to beg for the poison that had almost killed me.

With all the force in my chest, I screamed out what sounded no louder than a grunt when it, at last, came out: "Agua."

The sound of my voice shocked me, and everyone around me. It took the wind out of the room. Only the wall fan was stirring in the glacial silence. Everyone seemed frozen in place—as if in an instance of neglect a precious artifact had fallen and broken into irreparable pieces. The hush of death.

Maybe I had died and didn't know it? They drifted out of the room one by one in the funereal hush, except for the tall nurse with the black hair. Her nearness scared me now. She showed me a paper cup with a drinking straw and brought it to my lips. "Water," she said.

To someone without a past, the present floods in with a frightening effect. The ordinary becomes significant. I instinctively suctioned the water through the straw, forced my throat to swallow. My body reacted with horror to my first gulp. Some spilled out the side of my mouth and down my neck, cold. But the liquid I did swallow poured through my insides with a life-giving freshness, as if it were all I'd ever need.

From then on the people in white, nurses—what else could they be?—entered and exited the room with a more casual manner than before. The maternal tenderness I had sensed in them before no longer shone on their faces.

It came to me that I preferred it this way. Without knowing why I realized the less I saw of them the easier I felt. A few of the nurses I had seen hovering over me stopped coming. I avoided speaking, remembering the adverse reaction it had on them. Instead, I blinked my eyes in salute whenever they came near. Moaning and grimacing became my main means of communication when I needed anything.

What lay outside the doors became my main preoccupation. Witnessing what went on around me took up all my energy.

I must have been unconscious for some time when I saw the doctor with the hooked nose and the tall nurse standing over my bed.

"Hola, amigo," the man said. He sounded friendly but he wasn't smiling.

I blinked my eyelids. The nurse removed the sheet over my legs and they busied themselves doing things to me, some of it painful but it made no difference to them. They asked me questions I could not understand, even the ones in their broken Spanish. At times, I thought of things to say but it was hard to say them.

In the morning, a black-skinned nurse sat beside my bed and watched me having breakfast, the first time I ate on my own. The food was tasteless; sugar must've been in shortage. The man they called Dr. Michaels came in as I was eating. He pointed at my hand and said to the nurse, "He's a southpaw," as if it explained something. She nodded. I didn't know what any of it meant. He gazed at me for a spell, as though his work was done in my case.

New faces entered the room throughout the day. I felt safe in bed under the covers, distant from what was going on, even when they washed me. After lights-out, they left me alone for longer periods of time. In the dark, I drifted in and out of myself. Shadows woke me in the middle of the night. I wondered why they called me David. They thought my name was David. I had my own name. I could hear it in my head along with the echoes behind it.

In the morning, a new nurse woke me. She was standing by my bed taking my pressure. She introduced herself to me in Spanish. Her name was Maria, from Puerto Rico. The white cap on her wavy sable hair looked like a paper dove. She showed no expression when she changed me and removed the urine bag. She tried sounding cheerful, called me rubio because of my hair, she said. I wondered how I looked like, I could not recall.

Maria tried to engage me in small talk. It took a lot of me to utter a word, much less to sustain a conversation. I answered her with gestures and grunts. Maria told me the police would be coming back to interrogate me. They had come to see me some days before while I was still unconscious. The thought of it made me uneasy. Maybe she thought it would get me to say more than si or no to her. She asked me about a woman from Key Largo who had come to visit me.

"Do you know her?"

I shook my head a little. I had no idea what Key Largo was. It meant nothing to me.

Maria fluffed my pillow and pointed at the brown plastic button by the bed. "Use the buzzer if you need something."

So that was what the thing was for, "Gracias," I said as she left the room.

I don't know how much later a pricking in my arm woke me. Nurse Maria was back, this time with a different doctor, a well-fed man with a greasy face. She was in the process of covering me up again when the doctor pulled two chairs closer to me. He introduced himself in English. I forgot his name even before he had finished saying it—Mac something.

Nurse Maria took the chair next to his. The tall nurse I'd seen before remained standing by the wall, keeping her distance. The doctor spoke first then Nurse Maria addressed me in Spanish.

"His name is Doctor McKessy," she said pointing at the doctor. "He'll be your doctor from now on. And she's Nurse Angelo, whom I think you know." She paused and added, "Do you understand me?"

I nodded yes.

Dr. McKessy spoke to Maria as he looked at me. "He wants to know how you are feeling?" she said.

I felt my shoulder move up in a shrug.

"I think he'd like to hear you say something. If you can."

"Bien," I said.

"Good," she said to the doctor. The doctor gave me a nod of relief and spoke to Maria. She translated for him. "Can you tell us your full name?"

I couldn't think of it. It hadn't occurred to me to think of my name until then. If I had, I couldn't recall. Then, without any effort on my part both my first names and family names came clearly to me together with another even clearer feeling preventing me from saying it. The certainty that something terrible would happen if I did. I shook my head.

"You don't remember your name?"

I made a face to go with my negative reply, my first full utterance. "I think my name is David."

It made my interrogators squirm and scowl at one another. The nurse by the foot of the bed and the doctor spoke as if upset at some third person. Maria sat listening, looking out of place. The doctor addressed her and she said to me, "Are you sure your name is David?"

"I think so."

"Who calls you David, your mother, your family?"

"I suppose, yes."

The doctor spoke to Maria more intensely now and she, in turn, asked me a series of questions, one after another: "What is your mother's name . . . your father's . . . where were you born . . . where do you live . . . How old are you?" She waited for my answer after every question even after she knew my answer would be no.

The tall nurse stood by the foot of the bed, her arms crossed in frustration. She addressed Maria and then Maria said to me, "Do you know where you are?"

I said, "si"

They looked at me with a glimmer of hope on their faces. "Tell us," Maria said.

"I am in a hospital."

My reply needed no translation.

"Do you know in what country you're in?"

"In the United States," I said.

They spoke together as if I wasn't in the room. They weren't pleased with me, I could tell as much. For some reason, it distressed me. I am not sure why I felt I had to try to make them feel better. "Doctor, please," I said in English. My voice interrupted their debate. "I want to thank you very much."

They stared at me expecting more. But that was all I had. They continued talking among themselves, this time calmer but still dissatisfied. Something about me was not making sense to them. The doctor spoke to Maria. "What could you tell us about yourself?" she asked me.

"All I know is now."

My answer held them in an enigmatic silence for a moment.

Maria said, "You must remember something—your mother's name, your father's. You love your family, right? How can you not remember their names? Try—"

"I feel I do, but I don't. It feels as if it's at the tip of my tongue, like that. But it doesn't come. Sorry."

With a distinct tone of disappointment in their voices this time, they discussed my situation a few moments. The word amnesia sounding out several times. Dr. McKessy gave Maria some instructions and she repeated what sounded like a prepared speech.

"You can stop me if you don't understand me," she said to me. "OK?"

I nodded in agreement.

"You've been in a state of coma for seven days that we know of," she began. "If someone in our staff has addressed you as David, this is only because the hospital assigns a temporary name to patients whose identity is unknown, and solely for administrative purposes. We know this isn't your name—it would be an incredible coincidence if it were. We'll address you as David for the time being, until your name comes back to you—or the authorities handling your case determine your identity. As for your clinical condition," she said. "The doctor wants you to know the type of forgetfulness you're suffering is normal. It happens sometimes to patients who've been unconscious for a time, as you have. It's called post-traumatic amnesia—PTA—a temporary state during which you are unable to remember things that, well, we don't usually forget. Things like one's name—as it's happened to you. It affects everyone differently. But we're pretty sure in your case it won't last long. You're already aware of where you are. And that's a very promising sign. It means your memory's begun to store new events and recover past ones."

Maria listened to the doctor and added, "Yes. We're going to need to keep you here for now—for further observation. And we want you to know you can count on us to take care of you until you're well enough to move on with your life. However long it takes. Also, there are some formalities in cases like yours, legal aspects that are out of our hands and have to be taken care of." She glanced at the doctor and then at me. "But we'll cross that bridge when we get to it."

Dr. McKessy spoke directly to me apparently no longer concerned whether I understood him or not, although I actually thought I did.

"In the meantime, my boy," he said. "You've seen how the staff here treats you. You're in very good hands at the Jackson. Don't forget to mention it to your caseworker. OK? You are a very strong young man, and you will recover your memory in full very soon." Maria translated what I had already understood.

"Muchas gracias," I told her and then to the doctor, "And thank you, Doctor McKessy."

A surprised, approving grin formed in his liver-colored lips. "No problemo," he replied and walked away.

A minute later, I was alone in the room again. To know I'd been in a state of coma answered a lot of questions for me. But an instinctive fear, the type I couldn't question compelled me to keep my name secret at any cost. I had yet to recall, even have an inkling as to why it had to be this way, but it didn't matter. The feeling was too powerful to contradict. As for the rest of my memories, they could stay submerged in the black water where they had drowned that night of horrors for all I cared. Besides, what use could I have for any of them anymore?

In Miami, Miss Parker found a drive-in motel on Biscayne Boulevard. When she entered the room, the sight of it made her feel as if she had fallen to the bottommost of something awful. She felt martyrdom in her heart. She put her purse on the night table and switched on the air conditioner to clear the smell of disinfectant. Then she sat on the edge of the bed.

The previous night, when she had finally decided to go ahead with her plan, she became another person. She had closed her eyes and prayed as she had as a child and still believed in begging God to fix things was an option. In her prayer, she'd asked for a voice to tell her what she was doing was right. A voice was all she wanted to hear. She'd waited all night for it, and still, she waited. Sitting on the bed of the drive-in motel, she interlaced her fingers on her lap and prepared herself to petition God once again. But the room smelled so gross it embarrassed her to summon His name from there.

She knew there was nothing sane about her wanting to claim the boy, or that prayer could make it any rational. But she had convinced herself it was God's mandate she was following. Who else could be behind it? The boy had no one who cared for him, no relatives. If he did, they would've shown up by now. He only had her. And she wasn't about to let them shove him in some dreadful institution or an orphanage, a ward of the state, only because she and the boy were unrelated. She couldn't stand by and allow it to happen, knowing she could care for him as no one else would. He was already hers in so many ways.

She stepped into the cheap-smelling bathroom, changed into her nurse's uniform and tied her hair in a bun. She glanced at her wristwatch. When she threw herself into her plan last night, she had stood in front of the mirror and warned herself of the gravity of what she intended to do. She had to be thorough and meticulous as if handling a life-and-death emergency. She was aware that success would not be entirely up to her. The final decision would be the boy's—and, of course, that of God. The same way some medicines make you sicker before they cure you, she said to herself, sometimes only a sin can prevent a more terrible sin from happening. Perhaps this was how God had chosen to speak to her, with her own voice.

That evening, Nurse Maria woke me up and introduced me to the man in a suit and tie standing beside her. "This is Doctor Rivera," she said in Spanish. "He's going to speak to you."

They exchanged a few words before she left the room. Doctor Rivera, a heavyset man with sparse strands of hair on the top of his glossy sun-blotched skull, pulled a chair next to the bed. "¿Que es lo que hay, chacho?" he said as he approached me. He looked around the room and then at me, a grin playing under his mustache. "What's up, young man?"

His Spanish sounded a little like Nurse Maria's. He took some papers and a clipboard out of his briefcase. He flipped on his glasses like a man ready to go to work, every move he made accompanied by the heavy breaths of a smoker. "¿Como te sientes hoy? How are you feeling today?"

I nodded once.

He looked at me with the squint of curiosity. "¿Seguro?—Sure?"

I nodded again and he gave me a long scrutinizing look. "Mi nombre es Robert Rivera, PsyD, psicólogo del Condado de Dade," he said loudly as if I were hard of hearing. "I am the psychologist assigned to you by the Dade County Department of Public Health. I was sent here as a substitute for Dr. Rosenthal because of the language. Do you understand what this means?"

I nodded my head on the pillow, but I really didn't know.

"Can you, now?" he said. "The doctors here say you're all right to talk. Are you?"

I let out a hissing "Si."

"I want you to know one thing before we start, I am here to help you." He paused. "Do we understand each other? Yes, I see that we do. So, let me begin by asking you this: Are you being treated well? Do you like the people here in the hospital? Are they being nice to you?" His mustached grin widened as he waited for my reply.

I moved my head up down a little.

"You can speak freely with me." He paused and cocked his head. "Is there a problem with your voice? I see you swallowing a lot."

I mouthed no.

He crossed his thick legs and rested his clipboard on them. "Let's start with this: tell me your full name?" He looked at me with pen in hand, ready to write.

I experienced a flash of panic and closed my eyes.

"Bueno, chacho, what's the problem? Can you or can you not talk?" Dr. Rivera sounded annoyed.

It took another moment for my voice to come. "No se," I told him with a ghost of a shrug.

"Which is it, you don't know if you can talk or you don't know your name?"

"I cannot remember my name."

"You forgot your name?" He slipped his glasses off for me to see his eye-bulging expression of disbelief. "Can't remember your name? Is that what you're telling me?"

"No me acuerdo," I said. "I don't remember."

Dr. Rivera sat back on the chair, shaking his head, disappointed. "How can you not remember your name, for god's sake?"

"Me da miedo. It scares me that I don't remember anything—"

"Nothing, not even your mother's name? What did you call your mother?"

I gestured in the negative again.

Dr. Rivera gave me a long look. He didn't believe me—I could see he didn't. "¿Tu eres cubano, verdad?" he asked.

"Cuban?" I said, sounding as though I'd just found out. "Yes, yes I am."

"So, how can you remember that but you don't remember your own name?"

"Because Nurse Maria told me."

"She told you you're cubano?"

"She said she could tell because of my accent."

"You talked to her, then? What about?"

"About the things here—the food, the urine bag."

"What did you tell her that she guessed you are from Cuba?"

"She asked what I wanted to eat. I said frijoles—beans."

Dr. Rivera let out a single laugh. "I get it," he said—Cubans called frijoles what Puerto Ricans called gandules. "So tell me, where are you from, in Cuba—Havana?"

"Can't remember that either."

"Come on, answer this then: Do you like dogs?"

"Dogs?"

"Yeah, pets. You know, perritos?"

"I guess I do."

"So you do remember that."

"I'm not sure."

"So you don't like dogs."

"I didn't say that—"

He signaled me to stop and looked me in the eye. "I'll tell you what I think you are," he said almost in a whisper. "You tell me if I'm mistaken. Deal?"

I agreed.

"This is what I think you are: You're a refugee who escaped from Castro's Cuba." He shot me a knowing grin. "There are many like you around here these days. Does it come back to you now? How did you get here?"

I shook my head.

"I'll tell you how you got here. A few days ago, you and some friends of yours decided to escape from the communists in a boat—or was it a raft? On anything that floats. Right?" He didn't wait for my answer. "Where did you sail from—Varadero, maybe from Mariel? Then when you were out at sea, you ran into some sort of problem when the boat was near the Keys and it was either swim or die. You tried to reach the shore but something happened and you nearly drowned."

He bobbed his head sadly.

"But you were lucky," he went on. "The tide washed you ashore, unconscious. Or maybe you swam part of the way. You look like you can. Anyway, you ended up in the mangroves down there. Does that refresh your memory a little? You in that water, in the middle of the sea, scared to drown? Was that what happened? I'm pretty sure it was."

How did he know? "Was that how I got here?"

He didn't like my question. "It's you who's got to tell me." He sounded upset now. "Tell me. Did the motor on the boat malfunction? Did somebody throw you overboard and left you to drown? You've got to remember something like that."

"I don't."

"I have to tell you something, my friend," he said, shaking his head. "You're one lucky cubanito to have ended up here—"

"Where am I?"

He let out a mocking belly laugh. "Like you don't know."

"What is Dade County?"

"It's not Cuba. I'm sure you've noticed as much."

I stared into his dark brown eyes, biddy with condescension.

"I hope you understand," he said. "This memory loss of yours isn't going to fly for long. Real diagnosable amnesia is very rare in real life. I grant you may have suffered some memory loss because of trauma. But complete blackouts of the type you're exhibiting are unusual and short-termed when they do happen. Legally speaking, it won't hold water for long. But, listen, you look like a smart boy. Let me tell you something else." He rested his elbows on his knees and spoke very slowly. "The police, the FBI, and the rest of them are coming to see you pretty soon and they're going ask you these same questions. Don't think for a minute they're going to put up with your I-don't-remember nonsense. Do you understand me? Those master-race looks of yours aren't going to fool them—do you get what I'm telling you?"

"What do you want me to say?"

Dr. Rivera let out a long heavy sigh. He looked like he could use a cigarette. "If your forgetfulness goes on for a few more days, well? I wouldn't want to be in your shoes, cubanito." He looked down at the printed forms on the clipboard and wrote on them. It took him some time.

He was right. I did remember much from before the night the sea took me. I remembered my name. I knew who my mother and father were. I knew where I lived, and where I came from, could recite my address in my sleep. What compelled me to keep my name secret came out of a profound sense of survival I had to obey. I could feel its effect, but I couldn't remember its source. It was planted in my head like a piece of oblivion that told me to identify myself it would be the end of me.

Dr. Rivera looked up from his clipboard and asked me in a quick offhand sort of way, "What's your mother's name again?" I hesitated and his hand came up to stop me. "Right, you can't re-member." He slipped off his eyeglasses and bit on one of its legs while assessing my face. "Amnesia, huh?" He almost laughed.

He put his clipboard and the other documents away in his valise. "Well, Mister a.k.a. David Fine, or whatever your name is. If you're an amnesiac, then I'm wasting my time here." He stood up. "But hear me well, cubanito," he said shaking his index finger at me. "My guess is you're going to be institutionalized before this week is over. Do you understand what this means?"

He didn't wait for my head to shake.

"It means the county is going to lock you away in some convalescence unit with bars in the windows until we know who you are. After all, you may be in this country illegally. I'm pretty sure that's how it's going to go for you." On his way out, he stopped at the door and stared at me another moment. "Need anything before I go?"

I shook my head.

"Entonces buena suerte, chacho. Oh," Dr. Rivera said doing a double-take. "In case your memory comes back by the end of the week, tell Maria to contact me. And I'll see what I can do for you. You know, before they take you away . . ."

On Sunday evenings, the Jackson Memorial Hospital operated with a skeleton-staff. Except for the Emergency Room, all other departments were on weekend schedule. At dinnertime, only a couple of nurses stayed on duty on the floors. Nurse Parker knew this when she came in through the parking lot door at the rear of the building. Her heart froze when she crossed paths with Head Nurse Angelo and Dr. Michaels as they were leaving. But there was no way they could've connected her with the hair-soaked woman in the dripping floral dress who came to visit the boy that day with the uniformed nurse who marched past them with a determination in her face which no one would've recognized.

The hallways were at half-light. During her previous visit, she made a point of memorizing which stairwell and doors the service personnel and medical staff used. She went past the elevator doors and took the emergency stairs. When she reached the second floor, there was no one in the hallway outside his room. She opened the door and like a white phantasmal shadow slipped inside.

Her heart stopped when she saw he was not in his bed. She panicked for a terrifying moment until she heard a toilet flushing behind her. She wheeled and saw the bathroom door open and him coming out brightly. Face to face, she tried to contain what was evidently a mutual shock. He immediately hunched his shoulders and asked her help to get back to the bed, pretending to need assistance. She played along, wrapped her arm around his waist and sat him down on the bed.

She looked into his eyes looking back at her, both too shaken up to speak.

## FOUR

When I sat down on the bed, I looked up and saw her bright eyes fixed on me for what seemed a long time. I couldn't fit her in the scope of my present recollection. She looked different from the other nurses. Was she a new one? Her face warned me of something.

"Do you know who I am?" she said.

I almost understood her English. I felt I should say yes but said no.

"Well, how could you?" She glanced behind her at the door and then back at me. "Do you remember how you got here? How it happened?"

Although I sensed a recognizable quality in the deep, mellow timbre of her voice, I couldn't remember her. I shook my head.

"Like me to tell you?" she said. "I know how you got here." She waited for my reaction as though I should be intrigued by what she was saying. "I was the one who took care of you after they found you. I was the one who arranged for you to be brought here. I saved your life."

The last sentence I understood. "Save my life, you?" I said, hoping she understood me.

She remained silent for a moment, her eyes in slits of curiosity or surprise or mistrust. I couldn't tell which. "Where are you from?" she asked with a frown. "Your accent—"

"You say you saved my life?"

"Yes." She made it sound so simple, something she did every day.

"Thank you," I said.

"Did you tell the doctors your name, who you are?"

I closed my eyes. "I do not understand," I said, my English breaking as it hadn't before.

Her expression tightened for a moment. What was it about my voice that seemed to disappoint every other person I spoke with? She took a deep breath and tilted her head to one side. "What is your name?" she asked with a full voice.

I understood the question, having heard it so many times before. But in her intonation, it sounded almost menacing. "David," I said with the English pronunciation—Day-vid.

"Is it your real name?"

"Not sure. My memory is not so good. And you, are you a new nurse?"

My question seemed to renew the warm disposition with which she had come. "Yes and no," she said, taking my hand and caressing the side of my face. "I'll be happy to be your nurse. If it's OK with you."

Any form of affection when there shouldn't be any cautioned some part of me. But, not knowing what else to do, I went with it. "Yes, I'm happy too, yes."

A noise out in the hallway startled her. She let go of my hand and turned abruptly toward the door. When silence returned, she looked into my eyes with a grave expression on her face. "Did they tell you where they're taking you in a few days?" She spoke softly but emphatically. "Have they told you? Did the doctors say?"

"I do not understand," I said.

"You better. Because in a few days, they're going to take you to a place where they're going to do tests on you. Tests on your brain, tests of all kinds."

"Test me?" The idea scared the hell out of me. "What kind—"

"A whole battery of tests. Electroshocks—"

"But why?"

"To find out who you are and where you come from. To cure your amnesia and make sure you're telling them the truth. They don't trust you, David."

I looked away at the room. Visions of me shackled to a metallic table with my cranium cut open flashed through my head. "Tests? And this only because I can't remember my name?"

"They can do what they want with you. And they will. They can keep you as long as they see fit. And it's all legal."

I couldn't believe it. My head felt under attack. Where was I? "Test my brain only because of my name?"

"They either think you're lying to them or you need to be institutionalized," she said, pointing her finger at her temple. "Either way. You're theirs."

Then it hit me. Wait a minute, could this be Dr. Rivera's doing? Tricking me to find out whether I was telling the truth about my memory loss. It had to be. "If I can't remember my name it's not my fault."

"I know," she said. "But they have the authority to put you away forever if they want to."

My head kept shaking. I hadn't risked my life for this. That much I remembered. "Then I will run away," I said without thinking. I knew I could walk, stay on my feet. They didn't know I could. I'd known it since the day before. But where could I go?

Her demeanor softened the moment I uttered those words. "You don't have to run away alone," she said. "You could come home with me. If you want to."

I held my breath. "Please repeat this you have said."

"You can come to my home with me. It's up to you."

Just like that? "You will help me go away? To your house? Why?"

She smiled. "I have my reasons."

"But you work here."

"I am a nurse but I don't work here."

My mind was going fast and getting nowhere. "Why you want to do this?"

"Because I feel responsible for you. Because you are alive because I saved your life. Because in my home you will be safe," she answered, her eyes smiling.

"The doctors, they will know?"

"No. It will be our secret. I promise." She paused and stood by the door, looked in both directions, and came back inside. "Tell me, David. Would you like to come with me? If you do, you have to tell me now."

An electric current shot through my body as if she had offered me all I ever wanted. "This is possible?"

"Yes." She again looked over her shoulder at the door. "But you must do what I say. OK? And we must do it now. Right this very moment."

The part of my body that had been dormant until this instant cranked up to life. "OK, how?"

She had it all worked out. She pulled a pair of rolled-up mechanic pants out of her handbag. "Here, let's get you into these." She removed my gown and I fully naked slipped into the trousers. Nudity no longer faced me—by now half the world had seen me with nothing on. The pant legs were too short and the waist much too wide but she'd brought a knitted belt to hold them up. The rubber slippers clipped between my toes. Next, she handed me a white T-shirt with a car silkscreened on it and big enough for two of me. "Tuck it in," she said.

"Tuck? What is tuck?"

"Your shirttails, push them in your pants. You'd look neater."

Once dressed, she tried to comb my hair. I had to stop her. "Please, you're pulling it."

"Are you ready?"

"Yes, yes."

She took me by the hand and we slipped out the door. I followed her down the hallway I'd never seen. It was half-lit and deserted. We went past the elevator. She pushed open a door with an illuminated 'exit' sign in red above it. We crept down the stairs one step at a time, holding on the handrail. When we reached the landing, she told me to wait. She opened the door a crack and peeked into the main hallway. "Come on," she whispered. "Walk as normally as you can."

"Yes, I try."

It wasn't easy so she threw my arm over her shoulders and put her arm around my waist. The corridors were empty except for the sound of voices echoing from somewhere nearby. We moved on together. I got another whiff of her perfume. Two men, a nurse and a civilian, suddenly appeared out of nowhere.

They saw us but paid no attention to us. We waited by the Coca Cola machine and got going again when it was clear. All I could do was follow her commands.

"Now the hard part," she whispered in my ear.

We waited behind a glass door, then with an abrupt tug, she grabbed me by my arm and we hurried out to the parking area. My knees wobbled every few steps but she kept me upright. The faster we moved, the harder it was to breathe the muggy night air. We charged ahead past a row of cars facing a fence, my legs moving faster than I was moving them.

"Are you all right?" she kept saying and looking behind her.

"Yes, yes," I said. But I felt like vomiting. I would have too had there been anything inside me to throw up. I could not believe I was again involved in an escape in the middle of the night.

I didn't realize why she'd said this was the hard part until I heard her say, "They've seen us." Suddenly the lights outside the hospital switched on. Windows rolled open. We were almost reaching the street.

"Hey, hey, you two, stop, get back here . . ." we heard a man shouting.

"Over there," she told me, pointing at a red and white convertible parked beside the entrance to the parking lot. I heard her taking out the keys and unlock the car at the same time the man's shouting got louder. "Quickly." She helped me into the passenger seat.

More people came out of the back door of the hospital.

She started the car and drove off, tires burning. The car slowed down on reaching a multi-lane boulevard flanked by rows of palm trees and tall buildings. A left turn and we rumbled over a short drawbridge and into the dark of a two-lane highway.

I nodded when she looked at me in the glow of the car's dashboard. "I am OK," I managed to say, wiping the perspiration off my face. And I was OK, despite my trembling legs and arms muscles and my aching head. I felt alive, fired up. I leaned back on the seat and watched the night flying by, the wind of the living blowing on my face. The car, the motor noises, the tires rolling over the road, felt familiar, like a home-coming.

She asked me if I was hungry and I said yes. She was hungry too, she said. She then told me what I understood to mean that she had food for us in her house. I nodded my head again and she smiled. We said nothing for a while, both catching our breaths—mostly me. All the while feeling her presence beside me, her eyes in the dark wandering now and then in my direction, her hands on the wheel, driving whatever was left of my life as she was doing the car, her eyes wide, mad, happy.

I understood then that nothing would ever be again like before.

She said her name was Francis. Then she glanced at me. "And you are David," she said with a little laugh.

"Francis is pretty. French?"

"It could be." She smiled at the road ahead. "My full name is Francis Alice Parker."

"Francis, Alice sound good together. It has music."

"I'd never thought of it that way. You have a very good ear." She smiled. "Is nice to hear you speak. I could get used to it."

"It's very nice you do." I began to enjoy the calmed commitment of her soft voice. "You live very far?"

"About another hour away. We'll have plenty of time to make our acquaintance, if you're up to it."

We came across a few cars coming on the opposite side of the highway, but no car passed us. She kept a steady sixty-mile an hour or so.

We drove onto a bridge so long I thought it could reach all the way to Cuba. Beyond the guardrails, the night and the ocean fused together into solid blackness. The air grew heavier and humid like in the high seas. The saltwater air made me ill. I rolled up the window and closed my eyes, and rode on the drone of the engine, drifting in and out of consciousness.

"We're almost there," I heard her say after a while. "How are you feeling?"

"OK."

"What's my name?" she asked me, the light reflecting off the rearview mirror shining like a mask over her eyes.

I said nothing for a moment. Then, "You are Francis Alice."

"Just checking."

I realized why she had asked. "My memory is not so bad. OK?" I said.

"All right." She reached out a caressed my face. "That's good to know."

Human contact had its own stimulus. But I held back from reciprocating in any way. We weren't there yet.

The highway widened and we drove past a few neon signs outside closed shops, a filling station, and the incidental motel. She asked again if I was hungry and I said yes but was not. Well, maybe I was. "Do you like spaghetti? I could make you some when we get home."

I couldn't think of food. "Anything you give me is okay."

My answer made her chuckle. "I could make you bacon and eggs. I've got a few other things I can whip together."

I leaned my head back on the seat. At a stoplight, I heard the engine knocking while it was idling. I closed my eyes and had a vision of greasy pistons moving up and down in mucky cylinder shafts, lifters rattling loose, crusty sparkplugs, a motor beating out of rhythm, vibrating all around me. I pictured the tools I would need to fix it. It felt as if I had just bumped into an old friend. It distracted me from the feeling of nausea I'd been putting up with. The idea of making the useless useful again had a curative effect on me. It felt good riding in her Chevy. There was a lot I could do with it.

I opened my eyes to the night shadows flying by and the warm wind on my face. Her eyes wandered in my direction. She had the steering wheel in both her hands. Something in the composition of her face kept changing in the play of the light and dark of the road. She looked sad, she looked happy, euphoric, scared. At moments both despairing and ecstatic, her eyes sparkling with a smile that didn't show on her lips or vice versa.

The Chevy turned into a narrow street, an alley with no streetlights. The white graveled pavement crunched noisily under the tires, raising a trail of dust in the red glow of the taillights. A few low-roof houses silhouetted by the sides of the road inside the dark vegetation. "We're almost there," she said with an anxious look on her face.

I worked up a smile for her.

Going around a bend, she slammed on the brakes.

In the beams of the headlights, two uniformed men stood facing us in front of a red pickup truck and a cherry-topped squad car blocking the road. One of them made a hand signal.

Francis looked at me in shock, unable to speak.

Everyone who had ever meant me harm had come at me in a glinty-badged uniform. I could sense the ocean behind the shadowed houses. Voices rang out over the rattling engine. Francis opened her door and jumped out, talking, hollering. A shouting match broke out.

Charged by sudden onslaught of animal fear, I unlocked my door and slipped out crouching around the rear of the car and burst into the night, between two shadowed structures roadside toward the saltwater smell where the sea murmured. Quick, I looked over my shoulder and caught a glimpse of Francis Alice. She was standing in the shafts of headlights, her white uniform in the dust mist, her face lost in the dimness above it—looking for me I supposed. Maybe I was just hoping. The rubber slippers she'd given me were the first things I lost when I splashed into the black waters, then the oversized blue jeans came off with my kicking. My body began to tremble even before I became fully conscious of where I was again.

*What did I remember? All I remembered was water, animal water, burning into my eyes and nose . . .*

# Rhythm Guitarist

Maybe it was a case of stars aligning over Victor's Café or some other kind of magical coincidence, I found myself humming one of his songs at the exact instant Freddy pushed the swinging door and announced, "Guess who's here?"

I slotted the rack of dishes into the washer and looked at Freddy's grinning mustachioed face from across the steaming kitchen. "Cousin," I warned him. "You better not be joking with me."

He was about to answer when Alfredo, the old waiter, stuck his head in and confirmed it with his mocking high-pitch voice: "*Oye* Manu, I think the saints are on your side tonight. Your idol just sat down in my section. Want to work his table for me?" He cackled like a witch without waiting for my reaction and rushed back into the dining room.

I started to pace around the aluminum counter, drying my hands on my apron. Cousin Freddy watched me from the kitchen door, amused. El Maestro, the cook, was chopping something on the butcher block, peering up at me too, not so amused.

Freddy said, "He's here with his wife and another long-haired friend of his."

I stopped circling the counter. "Listen, Freddy, you will introduce me, right? You promised."

"We'll see how it goes."

"No, no, none of that. You said you would. Don't—"

"OK." He looked at me and then at El Maestro. "But you can't leave tonight until you finished. Everything cleaned and put away."

"Sure. Whatever you say."

"And don't forget this." Freddy cautioned me with his index finger pointing skyward. "These people come here because they know they can eat in peace and no one is going to hound them asking for photographs and autographs and the like."

"Yeah, yeah, sure . . ." I kept nodding my head.

"All right then," Freddy said. "If and when I see every-thing's OK, I'll bring you over to his table myself and intro-duce you. But remember: Don't overdo it. Understood?"

"Don't worry. I just want to ask him to sign my notebook of lyrics. Maybe shake hands—"

"Just don't forget what I told you. Is that clear?" Freddy wagged his authoritarian finger at me again so that both the cook and I saw he meant business.

"As clear as Varadero water," I told him. "But Freddy, listen, do you mind if I change out of these clothes? I don't want to do it dressed like this."

Freddy nodded his chin at El Maestro. "If it's OK with him; it's OK with me."

Wringing my hands, I gave the cook a pleading look from across the kitchen.

El Maestro looked at me, his Dixie cup hat down over his brow. "Bah, go ahead," he said with a downward wave of his hand. "Change if you want. As longs as they're working whites."

My hands began to tremble.

The main reason why I had accepted to work as a cook assistant—dishwasher and gofer-at-large—was because cousin

Freddy had assured me that 'my idol' dined at the restaurant on occasions. The idea that I could see him in person made it impossible for me to turn down the job, even though I hated the work. So for three and a half months I rode the subway downtown to 72$^{nd}$ Street, six days a week through the heat of summer and the fall rains, washed innumerable pots and plates worrying my idol might have lost his taste for Cuban food. But, at last, the waiting was over. And, sure, I was nervous.

I untied my apron and rushed to my locker. In the bathroom, I washed up and changed into clean, coconut-white whites from head-to-toe as if to attend a Santeria cleansing ceremony.

On my way out, I glanced at the calendar on the wall with the bikini blonde on the beach. I read the date aloud not to ever forget it. Friday, August 8$^{th}$, 1980.

When I looked at the wall clock above the calendar, my skin broke out in goosebumps. It was exactly eight p.m. on the eighth day of the eighth month in the eightieth year of our century. I felt my insides tremor; it was unbelievable. Eight was my number: the number of Obatalá, my Orisha saint. I just knew then that in exactly eight minutes I'd be shaking the hand of John Lennon.

Combing my hair in the washroom, I remembered John Lennon's number was the nine and that his father's name was the same as my cousin's—all trivia I was thinking of to distract myself from my other thoughts. Mental images I couldn't possibly avoid on a night like tonight. My memories of that season of horrors, which coincided with my discovery of The Beatles.

It happened during the 1969 sugarcane harvest. When the university closed down and so many students like me were forced into government workers brigades. A time I only wished to remember because of the dreamlike half-hour or so when after lights-out, a bunk-bed mate nearby played a portable cassette player he had smuggled into the barracks and we listened to The Beatles—batteries permitting.

In the stifling climate of those nights, the sound of their music had a spiritual effect on us, there was no other way to explain it. For a little while each evening, it made us forget our blood-blistered hands and tortured bodies after sixteen brutal hours of swinging our machetes in the fields. No one in our wall-less, mosquito-ridden dorm ever complained when their music played, not even the armed guard. The nocturnal noises disappeared, the impurities in the dark faded, the night became bearable. The mysterious fever that could drive even the strongest among us to lose it and take off running for the barbwire and into the deep shadows beyond from which no one ever returned aired away. When The Beatles played, we never lost any *compañero* to the fever and the darkness. And we were never lonesome. For this, I wanted to thank him.

I molded my hair over my forehead, looked at it, and combed it back again.

For me, it was more than the sound of their instruments and their reverbed voices, more than the simple meaning of their early songs, which I barely understood then because of my poor English. It came from some indomitable resonance that burst out of the tiny speaker in the cassette player, an electric joy, the roar of untamed love, the howl of hope. It had the effect of God on us, beyond the reach of the music. We talked about them in the canefields, debated the innumerable meanings of their songs, made up things about them. It distracted us from the pain while we worked. Sugarcane is a type of bamboo, a plant with blade-sharp leaves that slashed back at you when you try cutting them down. The 1-2-3 hacking motions with the machete—swing three inches from the ground, chop off the top of the shoot, shave off the leaves then throw the stalk on the pile—went well to the rhythm of some of their songs. Twist and Shout was a good one. It gave us the will to face one more day when we couldn't face another, to imagine a future where none was visible beyond the barbwire around the misery-infected labor camp.

Handling a machete didn't come instinctively to urban-dwelling students from the cities. But the Maximum Leader had said it was for the good of the Revolution, so we hacked and stripped sugarcane in the blazing sun in nonstop shifts of three hours, seven days a week until sundown. Guarded by armed men with the power to reduce us to animals.

Every day the brigade's infirmary was overwhelmed with every sort of laceration and nasty cuts, severed fingers and toes. I wouldn't dream of ever telling John of The Beatles any of this. I wouldn't embarrass him or myself with this kind of drama. Magical beings who live far from us mortals in their own mythological time didn't need to know that much detail. As with Obatalá, a respectful gesture of gratitude for the good they had done without even knowing was sufficient.

I don't think any of us ever thought of The Beatles as flesh-and-blood beings we could actually meet and talk with. In the slave-like conditions we lived in, I would've needed to have one lush imagination for that. To pray to them? Maybe. I heard of one of us who did. Rogelio was his name, a former altar boy. He prayed to John of The Beatles. No one had to ask him what he prayed for, we just knew. And his entreaty was answered, he went home with all of his fingers.

I gave myself a last look in the mirror and stepped outside.

"How do I look?" I asked El Maestro. He was chopping onions—my job.

He looked up at me without stopping his knife work. "You look OK."

I tapped his bulky shoulder. "I appreciate very much you letting me do this."

"Forget it."

"You're a good man, Maestro."

"I know."

The L-shaped dining room was half empty, as usual at that hour on Friday nights. I peeped from the kitchen door and there he was, his back to me, sitting at a table by the window with his Asian wife by his side. I had not expected his hair to be so light a color, nor as short as it was. He had on a dark long-sleeved T-shirt. His shoulders looked narrow, bony, but in constant motion as he spoke to the longhair man across the table.

I waved at Cousin Freddy and he scowled back at me.

"OK, OK," I mouthed and slipped back inside, holding my notebook of lyrics.

Eyeing through it, I remembered the night I vowed to teach myself to play the guitar as The Beatles played it. Two of my *compañeros* at the camp showed me the basic chords on a cardboard guitar neck, with the strings and frets penciled in. They said I had a knack for it. So that by the time I was trucked back to Havana and got my hands on a Spanish guitar my uncle had and never used, music became my reason for living.

Uncle's acoustic guitar was fine for learning but it wasn't the instrument a true Rock and Roller would play. It simply lacked the insolence and the fury of the electric. For years, I searched for one to no avail. In Cuba, it would have been easier to find a snow blower than an electric guitar, if you didn't belong to the revolutionary elite. Once, I even planned to break in the residence of Che Guevara's grandson who owned several, but my friends talked me out of it. Eventually,

I got my hands on a guitar pick-up and had it installed on my uncle's acoustic, which I had by then made mine. It allowed me to join a local band that played Beatle songs at house parties. Fulfilling my labor-camp promise remains my proudest personal achievement.

Cousin Freddy pushed the kitchen's swinging door. "*Bueno*, are you ready?" He looked at me, his mustached face grinning like a proud father. "Come on, let's do it now. They're done with the appetizers."

"Cousin, I'm a little nervous."

"Don't worry. You got a minute."

"A minute is all I need."

I walked behind Freddy and stood to a side when we reached the table. And there he was, no longer the round-faced youth of the album covers, but his unmistakable features, his severe lips, his projecting nose, his alert eyes, also lighter than I had pictured them, were undeniably him.

"Is everything to your taste?" Freddy asked the Lennons. "Did you enjoy the *tostones*?"

"Oh, they were all right," John Lennon said. "A little bit too garlicky. Didn't you think so, mother?"

"They were fun, I guess," his wife answered. "You know I like garlic. It's very good for you."

"They tasted nothing like bananas," the third person at the table commented.

"No problem," said Freddy. "I will bring you some without garlic sauce if you wish."

"No, no, it's OK," they all said.

Now Freddy glanced in my direction. "Mister Lennon, I hope you don't think it too forward of me, but if it's not too much of an intrusion, my cousin here would like your autograph."

Cousin Freddy took me by the arm and pulled me closer to the table. "Give Mr. Lennon your book. Did you bring him a pen?"

"Yes." I handed John Lennon a ballpoint pen and my ancient notebook I called my book of lyrics, stuffed with loose leaves written in different calligraphic styles. Freddy winced when he saw it.

Mister Lennon looked it over and said without me having to explain: "These are my songs in Spanish."

"My translations of the lyrics of your best-loved songs, yes," I managed to say.

"That's cool," he said. "They're not only my songs, but, hey—" He tried reading the text. "Oh, I recognize this one. This one is Imagine, right? Look everybody. *Imaginate*," he said, trying his Spanish. "And I know this one too. En Mi Vida. That's 'In My Life', isn't it?"

"Yes, sir."

"Look, mother," he said to Yoko, passing the lyric sheet for her to see. "My words translated into Spanish. Isn't the lettering nice?"

His wife glanced at the yellowed-out sheets and smiled, unmoved by it. It was reasonable she should be, I thought, considering his lyrics probably had been already translated into every language there was. But he seemed to be thrilled about it.

"Very good, my boy," Mister Lennon said addressing me. "Nice handwriting. What's your name?"

I told him and he autographed the first page of the book and the loose folio with the words to *Imagine* in both languages. "Here you go," he said, handing it all back to me.

"Thank you very much," I said, my head low so he would not see my eyes.

The longhaired man sitting with them at their table asked me if I was a musician.

"I am a rhythm guitarist."

"Me too," Lennon said delighted and shook my hand. "You know," he said, facing the others. "The role of the rhythm guitarist in rock is quite underestimated. No one understands how important it is anymore." He made a few more comments on the subject and turned to me again. "Do you have any more of my tunes translated into Spanish, in your calligraphy?"

"Sorry, I don't have the rest of them here." Actually, I didn't really have anymore.

"Oh well. Can you make a copy of these and send them to me?"

"It will be my honor."

"Drop it off at my office. You know where it is, right?"

"Oh, yes, we do," cousin Freddy answered for me. "Everyone here knows your building very well."

"You could leave it with José the doorman," his wife said.

I could have said so much more but I just thanked him again and stepped aside for Alfredo who was coming over with their main course.

I floated back to the kitchen.

Alone in front of my locker, I gazed at my book of lyrics with John Lennon's signature. A knot formed in my throat. The magnitude of the moment was too much. It just shot me back to those days that now no one wanted to talk about or cared to remember anymore. But it was inevitable, for me it was. Memory cuts its own pathways through the mind and the heart. And I could see every one of their faces again, my machete brothers, my amigos—for I still refused to think of them as *compañeros*—comrades—which was how our brigade commanders forced us to address each other as. One by one, they reappeared like in a black and white in memoriam film, smiling in their pain. I saw the *fidelista* police rounding us up like stray animals in the streets, wherever they found us. Why? Because we were easy prey. Because we'd grown our hairs too long, because our pants were too tight, because we play the guitar and sang in the park, because we banged on drums on the beach. Us, a generation beaten into slavery like the Indians and the Africans before us . . . But, man, if only they could've seen me a moment ago, sharing the same physical space, breathing the same air as that of John of The Beatles. The Rock and Roll angel messenger, the voice of the voiceless . . . "You say you want a revolution, well you can count me out!" . . . Oh, if they could only be here now and see it hadn't all gone to waste. I held the hand of John Lennon.

I allowed myself a couple of tears in honor of the occasion—my first ones since.

I put on my apron and went to the kitchen. I almost sneaked another look at him through the porthole in the kitchen door to remind myself it was true. Instead, I picked up a stack of greasy plates and slid them into the steaming dishwasher. I peered over at El Maestro and noticed him staring at me.

"Thanks again, Maestro."

"So when are you quitting?"

"What do you mean?"

"You've met your John Lennon. So when are you leaving the job?"

I smiled at him, realizing he must have overheard me grumbling the threat on some busy night. "Not yet," I said. "I like it here with you."

He flipped his spatula and slid it under a ration of *vaca frita* on the grill, the last order for the night. I don't think El Maestro believed me, but now I had other songs to translate and my calligraphy skills to refresh. A good reason to hang on at Victor's Cafe a while longer.

At half-past midnight, I helped Alfredo lock up the front door gate. Outside was muggy, steam shot out of a street manhole. I lit a cigarette in front of the bas-relief mural on the restaurant's façade. It depicted a bare-chested Cuban sugarcane cutter and a two-oxen cart in a cane field—Victor's idea of giving his restaurant a Creole touch.

"Have you seen anything uglier than that?" Alfredo said. I gave it my hundredth look. He shook his head with a humorless grin. "It's been here so long they'll probably make it a historical site."

I said nothing. For me, it already was.

# The Old Farts Tour

Friday, I got another call from Wayne with more news on the group. I was alone in the perpetual night of my studio listening to playbacks, surrounded by pilot lights, faders, and meters. Apparently, the agent he'd been talking to about a possible European tour had called him back with a series of engagements in Britain and Spain he had lined up for us. Wayne, hungry to hit the road, had been calling with weekly reports on the negotiations since our ten-year-old record album had been reissued as a CD. I had not given it much thought until now, thinking it would come to nothing, as usual. But it was for real this time, he said.

"Better start dusting up your gear, my man. We've got places to go and music to play."

"A hundred percent for sure?"

"I'll fax you the contracts and see for yourself," he answered with his cocky laugh. "Got to tell you, we've never been offered this kind of money before."

"Well, money isn't what it used to be either."

"Neither are we."

He got no argument from me.

At first, I had felt a little skeptical, detached about the whole thing. Going back on the road with the band would keep me away from my studio business, which wasn't so great but it paid the rent. It all changed after I played the digital remix of the original record on my home stereo. It sounded punchier, powerful, as close to studio sound as you could hope for. Even the songs I had hated before made me proud of having written them. And what was best, my wife, my toughest critic, agreed.

"Why shouldn't you be proud to play those songs again?" she said to my profound surprise. "Those songs are your children, your creation."

I remembered the lumpy feeling in my throat upon hearing her say it like that. I hugged and kissed her. I had never missed so much not having a child of our own before, hers and mine, a real child with whom we could share moments like these. "Yeah," I said as we lay on our couch. "It'd be a kicker to have a little one to play these songs to. From his dad's wild rock and roll days."

"Why would it be a he?" she said.

"Well, now." We cuddled tighter. "A girl would be nice too."

"Maybe we should look seriously into adopting. When you get back."

"It wouldn't be the same," I said, evading the issue. She knew how I felt about it.

"I think you could be just as proud of an adopted child as you are of your songs."

"You know I'm an old-fashioned boy, babe. I like to earn it."

She didn't insist. She never did. We fell asleep in each other's arms after another attempt at earning it.

The series of dates—for it would have been too pompous to call it a tour—were scheduled to begin in London, England, and conclude with a concert in Madrid, Spain, where for reasons unknown to the label, the group's CD had sold an incredible ten thousand copies in two months without counting bootlegs, calculated at another three thousand copies.

Rehearsals commenced in October and so did the arguments. The first crisis was a serious one. The problem was Wayne's chops—or the absence of them. He had quit playing drums three years ago and it showed from the start. Sammy's case was the complete opposite. To him, his instrument was his life and for some dreamer's reason, he couldn't imagine any musician being any different. He had never stopped playing and it too showed the moment he plugged his Fender Precision bass in his Ampeg amplifier. We said nothing to Wayne, only winced at each other whenever his dulled timing got in the way. We tried to ignore it, hoping he'd get his feel back.

As for me, I still remembered my parts pretty good. I had made them up and had played them in every state of consciousness and far too many times not to be able to fake them when my mind went blank. Still, it took several finger blisters and much pain on my shoulder (anyone who has ever played a Les Paul Custom for ten hours a day knows the pain I mean) and many broken .009 strings, before my fingers loosened enough for me to feel in full control.

By the end of our third full-band rehearsal, everything started to smooth out except for Wayne's timing problem. More and more I found myself worrying over every drum fill he tried, pushing us out of meter. I noticed the frustration building up on Sammy, having to keep adjusting to every time fluctuation. I knew our pampering silence would not last long. Even our hired keyboard player had started to feel free to make faces. But the band's rebirth had been Wayne's work and we, I, owed it to him to give him every break.

To avoid repeating past mistakes, I decided to bring it up before it got out of hand. So, after that night's rehearsal, I proposed the three of us should discuss it and find a solution we could all live with—hopefully, without too much pain.

It was cold and traffic noisy under 59th Street Bridge ramp. Sammy and I were leaning on his car parked outside Roxy's rehearsal studios. Wayne stood on trial before us.

I laid it out for him. "This just isn't working."

"What are you talking about?"

"Your playing isn't cutting it," Sammy said.

"Come on, what the hell is this?" Wayne looked about to snap back. Then, switching from Sammy's face to mine, he caught the seriousness of the situation. "Is it really that bad?"

"No, but bad enough."

"Why didn't you say something?"

"We did," I said. "But it got to a point that, well."

"We felt bad about it, man," Sammy said, grimacing as if it hurt him to admit it. "But your playing is killing me. You rush the tempo, make it drag. The click-track doesn't help you. It's messed up. I mean—"

Wayne glanced at me. "He's right," I said. "Don't you hear it yourself?"

"Hey Wayne," Sammy added. "You know I love you man, but it just can't go on like this."

I nodded my head in solemn accord. "We can't go out and play, not this way."

Wayne glanced up at the icy night, drew a long, sad smoky breath but did not fight it as we had expected him to do—as he would have with anybody else at any other time. To Sammy's and my surprise—and expense—he had already been thinking about it. He proposed a solution that we, just as surprisingly, agreed with in the interest of fairness: a second drummer.

"If it's OK with the Grateful Dead and the Allman Brothers, it's got to be OK with us. What do you say?" Wayne said. "Two drummers."

We agreed to give it a try.

A couple of days later, Wayne introduced us to our second drummer, a young kid from Jersey, a weightlifter-type with a great smile and furious chops. He came already knowing our material from a cassette Wayne had given him. The kid had a pounding downbeat that could tear down walls, and what was best, he made Wayne sound on meter. After rehearsal, we drove out to the Sage Diner on Queens Boulevard and held a little celebration to get to know the kid a little better.

Outside of certain details, there was little to know. We could see he was almost a replica of our hormone-rich selves when we started out, twenty-one and eager to start collecting on some of the fringe benefits of life on the road he'd heard about. Wayne advised him to stick with Sammy if he wanted to know how that worked. "But stay away from us," Wayne said, shaking his thumb between us. "Him and me, we got wives back home, don't forget it."

The kid bobbed his head like a boxer listening to instructions before a fight. "I'll be cool."

From then on, every crisis was infinitely more manageable.

The songs started to take shape. Having two drummers gave our show a thundering drive it never had. The kid's impeccable timing worked like a human click-track for Wayne to follow. It built up our confidence immensely. So by the time we did our warm-up gigs at a club in Long Island, we felt confident enough to work in some theatrics into the show. It ended up being our usual stage clowning and typical rock-guitarist choreography Sammy liked and I did with him mostly to humor him. Though not too much, either, I had to remind him. I thought a measure of dignity behooved us at our age.

"You've got to remember we're no longer a New Wave band. We're an Oldies Act now," I told him.

"Negative," Sammy said. "We're a cult band. There's a difference."

"We sure as hell aren't an Oldies act," said Wayne. "For that, we would've had to have a top-twenty song. Not just records bubbling under Top Forty."

"That's right," Sammy said. "Cult bands don't need no freaking hit records. We're goddamn rock and roll myths, ageless."

"Forever young," threw in Wayne.

"Oh boy," I said, laughing. "I think we better get some mirrors installed in this studio. Have you guys seen our hairlines?"

"So we're not thirty anymore," said Sammy. "Big deal."

"What do you mean? We're not even forty anymore." I had to laugh again.

From then on Sammy named our series of engagements The Old Farts Tour. But I had not seen him so happy in a long, long time, happy as we all were. And we had the right to feel this way too, for we were now twice the band we ever were.

We knew we had it right from the soundcheck at The Underground, our first date in London. We could hear it and see it in the usually unreceptive faces of the roadies and the jaded staff in the club. We packed the place up on both nights and the local rock press wrote some nice things about the show and us in the following days. A few famous rockers, veterans and up-and-coming, visited us backstage after the show, which boosted our confidence even further. They made us feel so good we disregarded our own transatlantic pledges and let ourselves be carried away by some of the after-hour craziness. We managed it well, though, every one of us. Besides, neither the times nor rock clubs were the same anymore. Women were fewer, drugs had gotten more dangerous, and sex could be lethal.

More dates were added to our mini-tour. We drove up to Glasgow to do a one-nighter and another in Manchester, then headed back north to Dublin, a Rock and Roll town as good as any. We never made it to Liverpool, to our letdown. Our agent couldn't get us the money we needed. Or so he said. We drove back to London for our remaining date, charged-up as we'd been on our first tour ever. It did not escape any of us how lucky we were to be playing those songs twelve years after we had recorded them. I remembered the conflicts, too. The one over who should be credited as the song composers. It may have seemed long forgotten now, but back then it was a low point for us. Maybe our lowest. It came from Sammy and Wayne's idea that playing the rhythm section on the record gave them a right to collect on the compositions as co-composers. I knew better but did not get in their way. They went to management with it and, of course, the lawyers straightened them out. It was a big one, and I the target. I had written the words and the chord progressions of the songs on my own, except for a couple of them, and stood by it. They hated me for a while, for not agreeing to register the songs under the name of the group—"like the Doors or Queen . . ." Rock and Rollers dreamed of everything, of a new instrument, a record deal, a Number One LP, of Rock stardom and its riches. Once it starts, you never stopped dreaming.

Even at our last night in London with the club half empty—because of a major soccer game scheduled at the same time—we played our hearts out. The crowd sang our choruses for us. Words only we had sung before in our shows and our records but had continued to play somewhere often enough for these kids, some half my age, to remember them and sing them back to us—a magical moment for anybody who has ever written a tune.

Barcelona came next. By then, we could do no wrong. On one of our off nights, Sammy and I did a radio interview, during which I was required to speak English through a Catalonian interpreter because Spanish was forbidden in the station. The city was in full swing in preparation for the 1992 Summer Olympics, still months away. We could sense the excitement of it as we drove along Ramblas, the heart of the city.

After a finger dinner of seafood by the sea, our radio host drove us to a club where the local Pachyderm distributor had organized a party for the band.

Wayne and the rest of the group were already there when Sammy and I arrived. We went upstairs to a private area where the club's manager and the record people held a toast for us. At some point, while the party was going, Sammy came over to where a local rock critic and I were discussing the 'roots' of our group's music. I had downed so many Mahou beers and been passed so many *porros* by then I was ready to talk with anybody about anything.

Sammy approached us arm-in-arm with a familiar-looking tall blonde, but I was in the middle of an important statement I wanted to finish making.

"Excuse me, Sammy," I said and addressed myself to the critic again. "That's not accurate. You can't say we sound like Springsteen on 'Edge of the Night' any more than you can say we sound like the Police on 'Elena' just because it's a reggae-like tune. It's not fair."

"So who inspired you on those tunes?"

"Well, the Bobs—Dylan on one and Marley on the other. The same people who inspired Springsteen and the Police."

"I think I understand what you mean now," the critic said. "But you must agree all art forms are rooted in tradition."

"Oh, I agree with that OK. I think it's inevitable."

Our Catalonian critic then turned to Sammy, who was waiting to get my attention. "And you," he asked with a scholastic air. "What is your philosophy of music?"

Sammy, a whole head taller than all of us, squinted an eye and rubbed his chin as if looking for inspiration. "For me," he said. "There are only two kinds of musicians in the world. Those who understand 'Louie Louie' and those who don't."

I nodded in profound agreement and so did the critic.

I turned to the blonde Sammy had brought.

"Don't you remember me?" she said.

Sammy flashed his rascally smile at me.

"Sure," I lied.

"What's my name?" she said.

"Ah gee, you can't hold me to that. I can't even remember my name. But I do remember you."

I kissed both her cheeks and as I did, I made a face to Sammy and he came to the rescue.

"Of course he remembers you, Julia," he said. "He's never stopped talking about you."

"You're such liars," she said with an even more familiar laugh.

I gave her a quick up and down and she came back to me. She was long-legged Julia from Amsterdam, the Dutch beauty who had traveled with me during part of our Europe tour in '82.

"My Julia, you haven't changed at all. I'm so glad to see you. How long has it been?"

"It feels like an eternity. Doesn't it?"

"Well," said Sammy. "I'll leave you two to your reminiscing. I got to get back."

"Sure, me and Julia got plenty to talk about."

It all came back to me the longer I listened to her. Particularly that Nordic goddess image of her dancing nude in

a smoke cloud to some Reggae music in a hotel room over-
looking the canal. A vision that stayed with me for so long
afterward. I remembered how ambitious she was then, too,
and how she tried for days to talk me into making her my
business manager. She was still interested in the business end
of the music, except from a more distant, academic angle. But
she seemed truly glad to see me. We ended up downstairs in
the disco area until we sneaked out and took a taxi to my hotel.

At the hotel, we went to the lounge bar for a drink. Before
picking up the glass, I took a deep breath and informed Julia of
my current status. Then I lunged into a pathetic little speech
on how much I loved my wife and how much I needed her to
be supportive and not challenge my will power until she cut
me off with a mirthless laugh.

"You're so silly," she said. "You don't have to worry. I didn't
come here for that. Your marriage is safe with me."

With that understanding, we headed up to my room to
smoke some of the Moroccan stuff she said I just had to try.
While I searched the content of the mini-bar, Julia took off her
MC jacket and went to work. First, she pulled two cigarettes
out of her pack and broke them open on the table. Next, she
took out her lighter, heated up a chocolate kiss-size piece of
hash into a gooey paste, and mixed it in with the mound of
tobacco shreds on the table. Then she brought out a sheet of
rolling paper as big as a paper towel and rolled everything
together into a gigantic trumpet-shaped joint that would have
been the envy of any Rastafarian. She lit it up.

"I have a daughter now," she said from behind a blue cloud
of smoke. "She'll be eight next month."

"That's wonderful, Julia. What's her name?"

"Sara—and she is beautiful, soft and brown like her daddy.
She's at my mother's house, back home."

"And daddy?"

"I don't know where he is. He lives in Amsterdam. He owns a coffee shop—well, he has two partners."

"You see him?"

"Sometimes. He comes to visit Sara sometimes." She stood up to make herself another Cuba Libre. "I have to tell you something," she said with her smooth white back to me. "I had to undergo an abortion after I left you—"

"An abortion? Come on, you're joking." Then, seeing her face, "Seriously?"

"Yes, about a month after you left. I had to do it. I had no other choice." Her blue eyes opened in preventive admonishment. "And no, it could not have been anyone else's. I only tell you this because I think you deserve to know. It would not be honest of me if I kept it to myself."

"Jesus, Julia, man," I stammered. "Why didn't you get in touch with me? Why didn't you call or write? Didn't you have my address?"

"I had your telephone number in New York, but I couldn't do it. After the decision was made not to have the child what good would it have done to call you?"

"You could've told me anyway. Hell, what good is there in telling me now?"

Julia turned around to face me. "What would you have done had you known I was pregnant with your child and decided not to have it?"

"I don't know. Maybe I might've have changed your mind. Maybe you would've had the child and I would've taken care of it. Maybe be allowed to be the father—"

"I don't doubt this is how you feel now. Except, back then I don't think you would have been a good father, or I a good mother."

167

"That's your opinion."

"I did it not because I wanted to, but because I had to. And I still think it was the best thing to do. Have you any children?"

"None that's been born."

"Oh, that is horrible of you to say." She took a deep breath. "Are you angry with me now for what happened so long ago?"

"No," I admitted. "I'm angry at myself."

"Don't be," she said, lying down next to me on the bed. "You must believe it was for the best."

"For the best?"

"Yes, for you and for me."

"I'm not sure it was for the best. It certainly wasn't for the fetus."

"Oh don't say that, please. It sounds awful." She stood up. "What would you have done if I had had the child?"

"Be the father, what else?"

"I don't think you would've been a real father back then. The distance between Amsterdam and New York was not the only problem."

"I would've been a father to my child, believe me. You don't know me so well—"

"I don't know you, period. This was also why I had to do it. And I am not going to let you make me feel bad now after the hell I went through in those days. You don't know me either."

I jumped out of the bed and stepped to the window to catch my breath. I was too stoned and too pissed and stunned and needed to calm the hell down. "Look, I don't blame you for anything. It's your body and you did what you had to do. But I didn't. Do you understand me? You didn't give me a chance. You should've told me."

"There was nothing you could do."

Outside the window, the lampposts cast long electric streaks of light on the Barcelona harbor. How old would the child be today? Almost ten years old. My god. I could have been a daddy for that long.

We said nothing else about it afterward. I fell asleep, thinking about it.

When I woke up it was dark and Julia was not in the room. I looked around, hoping she might have left me a note. I had no idea where to get in touch with her. But she left nothing. I went back to bed and thought about the kid I never had.

The next two days stormed by like in a dream. My most vivid memory of our Madrid concert was of us standing on the side of the stage, sweat-soaked after our second encore, listening to the rumble and clapping of the audience in the cavernous Sports Palace, while toweling ourselves dry and drinking from plastic water bottles. We could not decide on which song to play next. We had performed every song in our catalog. It put us in a delightful bind.

"We've gone down the list from top to bottom," Wayne said out of breath but smiling. Then, "Let's do 'Edge of the Night' again. They love singing along to that one."

"Nah," said Sammy barely perspiring. "We can't repeat songs."

"Why not?" Wayne said.

"Look at them," Sammy said, pointing at the crowd. "They want to rock and roll, man, so let's give them some."

"So what are we going to do?" The rest of us wanted to know. Personally, I was burning to get back on stage but drawn a blank, couldn't think of what to play after a second encore I'd never imagined we'd get?

Sammy glanced at me, a sly smile on one side of his mouth.

"What?" I said. "You want to do our old Rock and Roll medley?"

"No way," said Wayne. "We'll sound like a bar band." Then to me: "What do you think?"

"Why don't we just go out and ask the crowd?"

That was exactly what we did, and for the next half-hour, it became a request-and-play thing between the audience and us. We ended up having to do almost the show all over again.

By the time we were back in our hotel, I was feeling every one of my forty-three years. I begged to be excused on the after-concert merrymaking the promoters had planned for the band. To Sammy's amazement, I also passed on the two gorgeous madrileñas he'd rounded up for us. It felt like a long-standing tradition had come to an end.

I went straight to my room and collapsed on my bed. I could not recall those typical end-of-the-tour blues hitting me this hard before and this soon. I could not stop thinking of Julia and what it might have been, a boy, a girl? I couldn't get it out of my head. I called my wife in New York. It was nine p.m. there. She had that sweet raspy, sleepy voice of hers when she answered.

"What? Were you sleeping already?" I asked.

"No, I just fell out watching TV. Oh wait, it's after three in the morning for you."

"You miss me?"

"Yes, very much," she sounded delicious.

"Do you really?"

"Yes, of course. Is anything wrong?"

"Why did you ask me that? Everything's fine. We killed tonight. The crowd went nuts. They made us play just about every song twice. Would you believe it? Now everyone is downstairs celebrating, but I'm tired. I'm up in my room."

"That's wonderful. I'm so glad you called. But hey, if the concert went as well as you said, maybe you should make an effort and join them. It's your last night and you know how touchy Wayne can get."

"Nah. He's fine. It's OK. It's just—"

"What's the matter, sweetie?"

"Nothing," I said. "I'm OK, really. Babe . . . do you blame me 'cause we can't have any children?"

"What? What's this about? Are you all right?"

"I'm all right. I am, really. I just wish you and I could have a kid, you know."

"Me, too. You know that."

"Yeah, I know. I wasn't always this way. You know that, right?"

"Oh boy, you picked a hell of a moment to bring this up."

"Never mind, babe. I just wish I'd known you ten years ago.

"What happened, Sonny?"

"Nothing. I guess I'm just coming down from everything. I'll see you tomorrow. You'll be at the airport?"

"The flight is coming in at six o'clock, right?"

"Right, at six. Love you, babe."

"Listen, love," she said. "Why don't you go down with the others and get drunk? You'll have a six-hour flight to sleep it off later."

"You're telling me to get drunk? That's a new one."

"I'm just sorry you're feeling bad and I don't know what else to tell you."

"Ah, don't worry. I'm exhausted, beat. I think all I have to do now is put my head on the pillow and I'll go out like a light."

# About the Author

Born in Havana, Cuba, Nick Padron grew up in New York City. He studied writing at New York University. He was an RCA Victor recording artist and the creator of *Diablero,* a rock opera based on Carlos Castaneda's books. His television credits in Spain include musical director and cast member of the highly acclaimed, award-winning series *Esta Noche Cruzamos El Mississippi* and of many other TV productions. His short stories have appeared in numerous publications and anthologies in the US and abroad. He is the author of three novels, including *The Cuban Scar* and ABN Award finalist *Where Labyrinths End.*

www.ingramcontent.com/pod-product-compliance
Lightning Source LLC
Chambersburg PA
CBHW020020030726
47499CB00007B/2195